SANIBEL
ISLAND

UNDER SIEGE

SANIBEL ISLAND

UNDER SIEGE

EMMET SPARKS

TATE PUBLISHING & Enterprises

Published by Tate Publishing & Enterprises, LLC
127 E. Trade Center Terrace | Mustang, Oklahoma 73064 USA
1.888.361.9473 | www.tatepublishing.com

Tate Publishing is committed to excellence in the publishing industry. The company reflects the philosophy established by the founders, based on Psalms 68:11,
"The Lord gave the word and great was the company of those who published it."

Book design copyright © 2007 by Tate Publishing, LLC. All rights reserved.
Cover design by Jacob Crissup
Interior design by Kellie Southerland

Published in the United States of America
ISBN: 978-1-60247-760-5
1. Juvenile Fiction   2. Christian Adventure
07.08.09

WHO IS EMMET SPARKS?

Emmet Sparks is not really a writer...he's a story teller. Telling stories to his own wide-eyed children, sitting around the campfire, or while tucking them in their beds at night.

One fourth-of-July night, while telling one of those gripping stories at the campfire, his son happened to pick up a box which once held sparklers. At the bottom was written a word of caution. It said, ***Emits Sparks***. The young lad said, "Dad, what is Emmet Sparks?" The family all chuckled at how the boy had made it sound more like a name than a warning on the box.

The oldest child at the fire said, "Daddy you oughta write these stories down...and here's a good pen name for you. Sort of like Mark Twain...you can be Emmet Sparks."

And it stuck...and so this family story teller will forever be known as...Emmet Sparks.

ACKNOWLEDGEMENTS

With deepest gratitude to:

God, for the inspiration of this story

Elaine, Rebekah, Kristen, Benjamin and Kay for
never-ending support in persevering
to write this story down

Ginny Fleming for tenaciously encouraging me to
complete and see this story through to publication

The Boat CHAPTER 1

It was ten minutes after 4:00 a.m. as Eleanor Pippin slipped her feet into cool, damp beach shoes. For more than thirty years, it had been her routine to rise before the sun to be one of the first shellers on the pristine Sanibel shores. Overweight, fair-skinned with red hair, now only possible with help from her beautician, she rubbed her muscles and joints hoping to limber up a bit for the stooping and gathering. Even though it was more of a chore now to find nature's treasures left by the night's tide, Eleanor still cherished the thrill of a rare find.

*Perhaps a Junonia shell today…*She thought to herself

Dave and Eleanor Pippin had moved to Sanibel in 1968. The winters in Yorkster, Minnesota, had begun to take their toll on the couple, so Dave took early retirement to move to their beachfront cottage. Here the winters were mild and the summer breezes rose up from the gulf bringing relief from the heat. The Island was not as crowded then and the shelling was more rewarding.

There were no traffic jams, since only the few cars that came over on the ferry went about on the Island.

Everything changed after the construction of the Causeway. Three bridges with two islands linked Sanibel to another shore. Sanibel Island had a connection to the mainland now which brought more people, more buildings, more traffic, more regulations…but more life as well. While Dave didn't much like the changes, Eleanor loved the diversity of people, the convenience for shopping and a new sense of reconnection with humanity.

Dave was gone now. He had died in 1985 of a heart attack while out fishing with his best friend, Ted Ingstrom. Not being a religious couple, Eleanor had Dave's body cremated and bid a simple farewell out in the Gulf, strewing his ashes over the choppy waves. Alone now for nearly twenty years, Eleanor had continued her routine of shelling, cleaning, and creating masterpieces with her discoveries. She'd won a blue ribbon in every shell craft fair since the fair began many years ago.

This dark morning would be different. Her find would not be a treasured shell. In fact, it would not be a treasure at all. It would be a day Eleanor Pippin would long to forget but could not. It would be a day when all of Sanibel would be changed by her discovery.

The back door creaked and slammed against the door stop as Eleanor made her way down the steep stairs leading to the beach. With her radiant lantern in hand, she slowly made her way swishing through the sea grass to the shore. The tide was low now…just right for finding the best shells. Several live conchs squirmed about struggling…as if drowning in the morning air. As was her morning custom, Eleanor tossed a few back into the rippling tide and said, "Here's a second chance for you my friend," and went on her way seeking out vacant shells. A huge jelly fish washed up near her foot and startled her a bit. She'd been stung a few times and she didn't want that experience again. Not at her age.

The glow of the morning sun was beginning to illuminate the horizon. Even in summer, the moment before dawn is still the coolest time of day. But Eleanor welcomed the cool breeze, for she knew that soon the July heat would make the day just bearable in her cottage on the shore.

As Eleanor walked, stooping and gathering her eyes fixed on the jewels around her feet, she glanced up for just a moment to catch the sun breaking the horizon. That's when she saw it. Perhaps one hundred yards out...maybe not that far: Large, ominous, dark, mysterious...unlike anything she'd ever seen on Sanibel.

It was a boat. No small boat. Not even what one would call a large fishing boat. There in the dim light it looked like an ocean liner to Eleanor, but how could that be? How could a ship this size come to the shore of Sanibel?

Several things became clearer as the sun rose full above the horizon. It was not an ocean liner, but it was a large freighter. Obviously it had approached the shore during high tide and now was stuck fast on the sandy bottom of the shallow Sanibel coast line. She saw no crew. She saw no one at all. She simply stood there alone peering at this misplaced ocean beast nestled on her exclusive Sanibel Island.

The boat was covered with barnacles and rust. Eleanor found it amazing that the craft had floated at all. Looking at the gear and riggings she saw that everything was in disarray, as if the ship had been tossed about and slammed on the shore by some great wave. But there had been no storm last night...no turbulent waters. This damage had been done long ago, unattended in disrepair. Perhaps the boat had broken free in Hurricane Ellie that had plowed across Sanibel and Captiva last summer and had simply been drifting. Drifting for nearly a year...*Not likely*...she thought.

As the morning light became full and the shadows of dawn faded it was then that she noticed. Footprints...and not just a few...coming up from the water as though sea creatures had sprouted legs. It was difficult to determine how many people had disembarked the rusty craft, but it was clear there were many. A well-beaten path led into the dense underbrush taking the landing party to a place of hidden refuge.

As Eleanor peered into the underbrush, hoping to see no movement there, the morning breeze shifted. The Gulf air caressed the sullen ship and a stench unlike any Eleanor had ever smelled made its way to her sensitive nostrils. "Uck! That's awful!" She exclaimed. "That smells like death."

First Sighting

Ben Johnson had been a sacker at Hailey's Store for about a year now. He loved the work, especially meeting so many interesting people on Sanibel. The tips came in handy too since he was saving up to buy a car. You see, Ben was at an awkward age. As a six-foot-tall fifteen year old, he felt he was too old to be biking all over the Island, but he was still too young to drive.

Ben had biked on every inch of the Sanibel bike paths, as well as exploring uncharted territories. He'd had several years to do that. Ten years earlier, Ben's dad, Tom Johnson, had been called to serve as pastor of the Community Church. So at the age of five, Ben came with his parents, three sisters, two dogs and two cats to Sanibel Island.

It was in the first grade that Ben and Justin Marks became best friends. The friendship started when the two of them got in trouble together for sneaking a tree frog into Elizabeth Gurner's lunch box. They sat together squirming in the Principal's office, certain that their offense would lead to life altering consequences...perhaps prison. Fortunately, the principal had mercy on them; one week of detention after school helping the custodian empty trash cans. It was during this week of walking through the empty halls of Sanibel Elementary, disposing of wadded up notes, tests, and Kleenexes that Ben and Justin became fast friends.

As the boys grew, they found their greatest adventures: biking, rollerblading and kayaking around the Island. As they rumbled about the tropical paradise they became familiar with every inch of its beautiful terrain. They knew where to spot the most fascinating wildlife…as well as many great places for adventure and private hideouts.

Ben and Justin had seen many things unnoticed by everyone else. Like the time they saw the Jamaican workers eating out of the dumpster behind one of Sanibel's finest resorts. And then there was that early morning encounter just prior to an exquisite Sanibel sunrise when they saw four dark cars parked near the pier. A cluster of men dressed in dark clothes were exchanging comments, as well as something in a paper bag. One man was holding something that looked like a gun. Most vivid in their memory was the steamy afternoon they saw a twelve foot alligator launch out of the water like a torpedo and drag a curious raccoon to its death into the dark pool. They had been moving toward the coon themselves and were only about ten feet away when the surface of the water broke with a blast.

They had seen a lot. Many of their memories gave them chills as they discussed them weeks, months, and even years later. But for Ben Johnson, all of the past adventures would pale to the encounter he would have this night. The fear he felt at the water's edge that hot afternoon with the alligator would seem like nothing compared to the terror that would soak to his soul tonight.

9:00 p.m. was quitting time for Ben. He walked back

to the stock room of Hailey's Store savoring the smells of breads, dried cereals and fresh fruit. The ancient time clock that hung by the large back door was waiting to receive his time card...freeing him to head home for the day. Ben punched out for the day, hung his apron by the clock and gave a friendly goodnight to Dan Hailey, who was locking up for the night.   "Goodnight Ben." Dan Hailey said warmly. "You be careful tonight Ben. A strange boat came on shore down by Eleanor Pippin's place this morning. It looked like someone came on shore, but no one's been spotted. It's just odd. So be careful."

"What kind of boat was it, sir?" Ben asked curiously.

"They're not sure. It's an old rusty freighter. It's not an American ship so they're waiting for the F.B.I. to come to board her. It won't be until then that we know for sure just what kind of ship it is."

"That's exciting! I think I'll ride my bike down toward the beach and take a look!"

"Oh, I wouldn't do that." Dan cautioned. "The whole area has been roped off anyway. You couldn't get very close. Besides, it's not safe to be riding around that area after dark with who knows what's going on! Just go home Ben. I'll call your folks and tell them you are on your way."

"Yes sir." Ben replied with deep respect. "I'll go straight home. You be careful too Mr. Hailey. I'll see you at 1:00 p.m. tomorrow."

"Alright son. Good night then. See you tomorrow."

Ben swung his long leg over his bike and began the journey home. Decades before the Johnsons came to Sanibel, the city fathers had determined that the island should not have street lights. It was to be a nature sensitive refuge. Too much light on the island could confuse the hatchling sea turtles, who were attracted by the moon's light to make their trek toward the sea, not toward a well lighted center of town. Because of this commitment, the island was very dark. The light on Ben's bike was small, only lighting up the path about six feet out in front of him. It actually served more to be seen by others than to help Ben see. Still, he was glad he had a light.

The summer breeze blew gently as Ben sped down the winding paved bike path. The usual island sounds of bugs and birds filled the air. In many ways it was much like any other summer Sanibel evening, but tonight, Ben Johnson pedaled a little faster than normal…and because of that…and because of a growing sense of danger, Ben's heart pumped a little faster as well.

What was that on the path about fifty yards up ahead? In the shadows of the palms and pines Ben thought he saw something…or someone move off of the trail. His bike light gave no help, and the moon shed only about one fourth of its light. At least Ben had some light… some help from the moon to pierce this wretched darkness that seemed to be engulfing him now.

He slowed the pace as he approached the area where he had seen movement. As he peddled lighter his heart pounded harder…but he had to know if he truly had seen someone. At that moment, just as he came to the huge Australian pine where he thought he'd seen someone…or something…his eyes fell full gaze on two dark figures that lurked in the brush just ten feet off the trail. Two men, or at least he thought they were men. They looked more like skeletons with taunt leather hide pulled over their frames. They stood motionless before him. Ben slowed almost to a stop, straining to make out details of the sinister pair, but he couldn't tolerate the glare of their piercing eyes. He thought to himself… *Two gaunt demons from hell have met me on the trail tonight.* As Ben passed by them, neither figure moved. They simply glared at him with those evil eyes. While the two took no steps to harm the boy, he felt as though he had had a brush with death.

As if coming out of a nightmare into reality, Ben found himself peddling as fast as he could. His heart throbbed, his lungs burned, his legs ached as he turned the corner into Palm Ridge Courts. Not much further to home now…where there would be light…and safety.

At the kitchen table sat Tom Johnson, Ben's dad, weary from a full day of pastoring. Tom had only been home about twenty minutes. He'd had time to get a bowl of cereal, sit down with the mail and begin to unwind from a long day that concluded with a lengthy Church Council meeting. Community Church had been growing and needed to expand. Tom and the church Council had found that securing new land was difficult, but getting permits to build was an even greater challenge. On this warm summer night, Tom thought to himself…*It would take a miracle for our hopes and dreams to come to pass.* And at that moment he looked heavenward and said, "And that's right where all this belongs. In Your hands, waiting for a miracle."

No sooner had Tom uttered the word miracle when Ben Johnson burst into the house gasping for breath, panting out pleas for help, begging his dad to call 911. Tom had never seen such fear in the eyes of his son. All the noise brought the rest of the family into the chaos. The dogs were barking. Ben's sisters, Becky, Chris and Marty were shooting off questions like bullets from an automatic rifle. Mary Johnson, Ben's mom, just came and held her son as he gasped to get his breath.

"Hold on son. Just calm down." Tom encouraged.

"Easy son. Easy. Take deep breaths. Everything is going to be alright. Mary consoled.

"Sit down here, son, and get your breath. Don't try to talk. Breathe easier son.

Everything is alright." Tom said with assurance.

But everything wasn't alright. Little did Tom know… or anyone else for that matter, that as the Johnson family clung to one another in the safety of their well lit kitchen, sinister dark figures were lurking in the night all across their paradise island.

Missing

CHAPTER 3

No one in the Johnson home slept well that long summer night. The unknown has an element of terror about it that is hard to describe. What...or who had Ben seen on the bike path that dark night?

The morning sun was a welcome sight. It was as if now it was safe for the Johnson children to fully fall asleep—and they did. Tom and Mary sat at the kitchen table with their Bibles, a strong cup of coffee, hands clasped, praying for wisdom and guidance for the day.

Ben had told them of his encounter on the path, but they weren't sure what to make of it. It was dark. Ben had heard about the freighter on the shore...and perhaps... just perhaps, his imagination had run wild with him. It might have been nothing really—just two men out for a walk on a summer night. But Tom and Mary had never seen their son so wild-eyed, so filled with fear. They had called the police more to appease Ben than to issue any kind of serious report. After all, the two dark figures on the path had not done anything that could be described as threatening. Still, deep down, Tom and Mary knew that this event was not merely a teen's delusions.

The silence of the summer morning was broken by the ringing of the Johnson's phone. "Hello, Tom Johnson speaking."

"Tom, this is Pete. Have you heard the news?"

Peter Kinard was a kind, gentle man…a real pillar at Community Church. He'd lived on Sanibel Island for about twenty years now. He'd been an obstetrician before retiring, boasting of having brought over 5000 babies into the world during his long, successful practice. Even though Pete was retired, he continued to be vibrant and active, especially in the life of Community Church.

"What news?" Tom asked.

"The Island is buzzing, Tom! Strange things are happening all over. I spoke with Mayor Todd just a few minutes ago, and while they are trying to keep people calm, you can tell that they're afraid."

"Afraid? Afraid of what?"

"That's just it," Pete said softly, "they don't know what."

"Pete, you're sounding so mysterious. We need to talk. Can you and Sarah come over for coffee and fill us in? We've got a congregation to care for, and if there is danger we want to help in any way we can."

"You're a great pastor, Tom. Just like always, you're thinking of your flock. Sure, we'll come over. We'll see you in about half-an-hour."

Tom and Mary hustled to get dressed, straightened the house a bit, and put on another pot of coffee. Mary had a can of those "pop-out" cinnamon rolls that are ready and delicious in just ten minutes. As she struck the counter's edge with the can, the loud "pop" caused Tom to jump as if he'd been shot.

"Mary! You nearly scared me to death!"

"Sorry Tom. I guess we are all sort of edgy."

"I'll say. All this mystery is just so unnerving."

Tom walked over behind Mary, slipped his strong arms around her waist and gave her a gentle hug. "I know everything will be alright. God is with us and the light of His truth will shine on this whole mess in a matter of time."

Just as Tom was preparing to give Mary a good-morning-kiss, the door bell rang. With that the dogs began to bark, but this time the children slept as silent as stones.

"Hush up puppies! It's Pete and Sarah. Settle down and go back to bed." Mary consoled the dogs. After presenting a tail-wagging greeting to the Kinards, the dogs slipped back to the bedrooms to be near the children.

"Pete, Sarah, it is so good of you to come." Mary said. "We'll have hot cinnamon rolls in just a few minutes... and the coffee is fresh."

"Oh Mary, you shouldn't have gone to all that trouble." Sarah chided. "I know we've all had a long night."

"I'm glad you went to the trouble Mary." Pete grinned. "A hot cinnamon roll sounds like just what we all need."

As the two couples stood gazing at each other in the sun lit kitchen, they all were struck by the weariness, the apprehension—yet an overwhelming sense of peace that permeated their bodies and minds. The Kinards were good friends. Not every Pastor and his family are blessed to have such good friends. It was good to be together at a time like this.

Mary sat the cinnamon rolls on the table while Tom poured four piping hot cups of strong coffee.

"Tell us Pete. What is going on? What do you and Sarah know?"

"First of all, as I said on the phone, none of us really knows much for certain. The police are working hard to begin to put pieces together, and later today the F.B.I. will arrive to launch a full investigation."

"The F.B.I.?!" Mary nearly shouted.

"Yes, Mary. It seems this thing is being considered an international incident. Tom Rhodes, director of Homeland Security gave a statement on C.N.N. early this morning. He's sending in a special task force as well."

"So, what are they investigating? What's happening? Mary said anxiously.

"Ben said something about a ship…an old ship stranded on the beach down by Eleanor Pippin's. Is that what they're investigating?"

Sarah piped in at this point. "Yes, it appears to be an old freighter. No one's gone on board yet. They're waiting for the F.B.I."

"But there's much more than an abandoned ship. There were footprints. Hundreds of them! They came on shore near the ship and led into the underbrush. Someone has invaded our Island." Pete explained.

"Someone is on the Island from that ship? But who and why?" Tom questioned.

"That's what we're all hoping to find out soon. Bizarre things have started to happen with no clear explanation."

"Like what?" Mary asked.

"Tell 'em about the rabbits, Pete. I think that is so strange." Sarah interjected.

"You remember how the Wyckoff's raise those pet rabbits behind their house over in Harborside Court?"

"Sure." Tom and Mary said in unison.

"Well, eight of them were gone this morning. No one heard a sound. The dog didn't even bark. It was as if they simply vanished from their cages. All of the doors were latched, and nothing else seemed disturbed."

"That is strange." Tom said. "I'm sure the Wyckoff children are very upset."

"There's more, Tom. Tell them about Mrs. Miller's Cadillac, Pete."

"You remember Gurney Miller, the widow who lives down on Fig Lane. She has that '83 Cadillac that has only 11,000 miles on it...or I should say, she *had* an '83 Cadillac."

"No way! It's gone?" Tom exclaimed.

"Just as if it floated off the property. No one heard a sound—and she had an alarm system. Poor old soul. She left the keys in it just like she does every night, but it doesn't seem anyone drove it away last night. The way that engine roars, the whole neighborhood would have heard it."

"This is all so strange...so eerie."

"That's not the worst of it, Mary." Pete's face grew deeply serious and Sarah became very still.

"Someone broke into Lawrence O'Malley's place."

For several moments no one said anything. Lawrence O'Malley's place was a virtual fortress. He was an eccentric millionaire who relished exotic collectables, went wild game hunting in Africa and kept a thousand secrets from all of Sanibel. There were jokes about O'Malley's mansion, with rumors that rounded the Island each time Mr. O'Malley made a stop on Sanibel from one of his world tours. No one really knew what all he had in that house. Only a few folks had ever entered, and most of those were repairmen or cleaning aides.

Pete went on. "A neighbor saw the front gate open and went up far enough to see that the front door was open as well. He called thinking Mr. O'Malley might be home, but there was no reply. He then called the police."

"What did they find?"

"The place had been ransacked. Many of Mr. O'Malley's

fine collectables were destroyed. At first they couldn't tell if anything was missing, but when they entered the big game room, they all stopped in their tracks."

"Oh Peter. What was it? What was gone?" Mary pleaded.

"Guns. All of O'Malley's gun cabinets, and cases of ammunition were gone."

"Oh, no!" Tom exclaimed. That's horrible!"

"It's worse than that, Tom. When they went to the store room they found four empty crates. Crates that once held...dynamite!"

The Sanibel Police

Officer Schmidt had been with the Sanibel Police Department for fifteen years. Not only was he an outstanding officer, there was hardly a finer man on the Island. He loved the community, especially the youngsters. His favorite assignment on the force was the appointment as the D.A.R.E. officer at Sanibel Middle School. While drugs were never a major problem on Sanibel, awareness education provided a healthy deterrent to keep it that way. Officer Schmidt was perhaps the greatest asset to the program because every kid on Sanibel loved and respected him.

Maybe that's why they sent Officer Schmidt to the Johnson's home that day to interview Ben. What Tom and Mary thought might have been a frightened teen's exaggerations, the Sanibel Police was taking as serious hard evidence in a very perplexing situation.

"So, Ben, can you describe who or what you saw near the bike path last night?" Officer Schmidt said gently.

"It was so dark sir. But...I do remember those eyes.

They were eyes that looked right through you. They were dark eyes. Desperate eyes."

"What do you mean by *desperate* eyes?"

"They looked hungry, angry and frightened all at the same time. They caused a chill to run through my entire body."

"Now Ben, think hard." Officer Schmidt prompted. "What else did you notice? Surely you noticed more than their eyes."

"I did notice that both men were so thin. They looked like bones covered with dark, shiny skin. Neither one had on a shirt. I remember now...their ribs. They looked like the men you see in the pictures of the German prison camps."

"You said they were dark, Ben. Were they black men?"

"Yes. Yes they were. Very black."

"Ben, everything you tell us is helpful. Is there anything else?"

Ben thought for several moments. "The smell. I remember a horrible smell. It smelled like the dumpster behind Hailey's store when it's got meat that's gone bad. It smelled like death, Officer Schmidt."

The room was very quiet. Tom and Mary had been there surrounding their son with encouragement. Becky, Chris and Marty had obediently remained in their rooms, but were listening intently through a crack in the door. A hush came over the whole house.

Tom spoke next. "Officer Schmidt. Who or what do you think we are dealing with?"

"We don't know, Pastor Tom. We've got lots of people to talk with today. While Ben is the only one who has actually seen anyone, there are odd things happening all over the Island. Mayor Todd is preparing to declare a state of emergency and call in the National Guard. It is all so mysterious. Hopefully today we'll get some answers when we explore that old freighter. For now, we all must be cautious."

"Mary, go get the girls please." Tom directed. "I think we need to talk a bit."

Mary went to the girl's rooms and found them each leaning close to the door with their ears perked to the conversation.

"Girls, come on in. Dad and Officer Schmidt want to have a word with all of us."

Officer Schmidt greeted the girls warmly then said, "I'm sure you know about as much as anyone about what's going on. We know just enough to know we need to be careful. Don't go off alone at any time. Keep the doors and windows locked. If you see or hear anything, call us right away.   Pastor Tom, I think you should take Ben to work today. I don't want him on that bike path alone, even in the daylight."

"Sure thing, Officer Schmidt. I planned to do that."

"As you all know, this island has plenty of hiding places. With acres and acres of conservation land and with all of the empty condos and homes right now, it will be a huge undertaking to find who has come on to our island."

"Has anyone been to the church today to check things out there?" Officer Schmidt questioned.

"Why no. It's Saturday. The offices are closed and usually things are quiet on Saturday morning."

"Tom, I think we'd better go check it out. Just a precaution."

Officer Schmidt encouraged Mary and the Johnson children not to worry. He seemed confident that they would unravel the mystery soon and that peace would be restored to the island. With that, he and Tom hopped in the Sanibel patrol car for the short trip up to the church campus.

As Tom and Officer Schmidt climbed out of the car, everything seemed alright. The lawns had been groomed to perfection by faithful volunteers. The courtyard was hospitably prepared for the coffee hour the next morning.

"Let's check out the Sanctuary first." Tom said.

"Sure. Let's go."

The Community Church Sanctuary was one of the oldest buildings on the island. Even though it had been expanded with three renovations since the original structure, it all had that wonderful fragrance of "old" and "comfortable." It had truly served as a sanctuary of hope on this sanctuary island for thousands of tourists as well as a solid core of year-round residents.

The church had marked its centennial anniversary just two years earlier with a celebration and picnic the islands would long remember. Former pastors came, the choir sang, but the highlight of the day was when ninety-eight-year old Hiram Holman told of his baptism eighty-six years ago by the first full time pastor of Community Church.

As Tom and Officer Schmidt walked up the center isle of the simple, but sacred house of God, they passed the dark heavy pews that had been salvaged from the very first church on the island. These pews, now nearly 150 years old survived Hurricane George. The entire island had been submerged, with the Church on the Rock, Sanibel's first church building, totally destroyed by the powerful surge.

"Everything seem in order here, Tom?" Officer Schmidt asked.

"Yes. It all looks fine."

The two walked throughout the church buildings, checking the fellowship hall, church offices, class rooms, nursery…even the restrooms. Everything seemed undisturbed. All was well. At least all seemed in order…until they came to the church kitchen.

Community Church had a large semi-commercial kitchen big enough for serving up fellowship dinners for several hundred parishioners. With a large freezer, foods were stored up for meals yet to come. Pots the size of five gallon buckets were organized neatly along the north wall, right next to the rack of butcher knives used for preparing vegetables or carving meat. Well, at least the pots used to be organized neatly. Not today. The kitchen was in shambles. Broken dishes covered the floor. Flour and sugar had powdered everything in the room. The large pots were in a heap now. Not one remained it its assigned place. And every knife was gone.

Officer Schmidt pulled out his cell phone and called the station. "You'd better send some support staff up here to Community Church. There's been a break in and some things are missing. We'll need detectives, sir. I'm sure we'll be able to get some prints."

As Officer Schmidt clicked off the cell phone, he and Tom both noticed the large freezer. The door was slightly ajar, with a chill of air spilling into the room. As Tom pulled back the door the two men peered into the empty freezer in amazement. Hundreds of pounds of meat, vegetables and frozen leftovers were gone…but where? And who took them?

What a day it had been. It was as if Sanibel Island had become a war zone. Sirens rang through the air several times each hour as new discoveries came to light…yet still, no one saw anyone. Only Ben Johnson had seen anyone suspicious, and there was still no hard evidence the two dark figures on the trail that night were connected to the crime scenes.

There was still no report about the freighter ship. The Mayor was to give a statement in the morning. Perhaps then the mystery would begin to become clear. Perhaps not.

As the Johnson family prepared for bed that Saturday night they were anxious, yet hopeful. They were all very weary. They had not slept well for a couple of days now and the stress was taking its toll. They gathered in the living room to pray for the island people, for the police and other emergency personnel. They were praying for the truth to be revealed and the frightening mystery to be solved.

Tom, who had planned to preach the next morning on the Parable of the Sower knew a more relevant message was needed. Meticulously he looked through the Scriptures, marking each verse that contained "fear not." He knew this was a word his congregation would need to hear.

As Tom and Mary kissed the children goodnight, they were glad that their oldest daughter, Becky, was home for a few weeks for the summer. Becky had a way about her that brought calmness to the other children. She was now a sophomore at Trinity Eastern in Vermont, preparing to be a children's worker in the mission field. In just three weeks she would head to Jamaica for a four week Mission Trip, ministering to people who had been hit by the same hurricane that struck her own home just last summer. They were rebuilding their schools finally after months of clean up…and she was excited to help.

"Mom…Dad…I know everything will be okay. Even though we don't know what's going on, God does. We must simply trust Him."

That's the kind of faith Becky had demonstrated from the day she surrendered her life to Christ at the tender age of ten. She'd always had an unusual maturity that must have been a gift from God. Tom and Mary found comfort in her words and assurance in her calming confidence in Christ.

As they turned off the lights and said their goodnights, there was a sense that the new dawn…the Lord's Day…would bring new hope. But it wasn't to be. Not yet. As Becky lay there in the dark, trying to drift off to sleep she sensed that someone was watching her. It was like that uncomfortable feeling you have when you just know that someone behind you is staring at you, but you dare not turn around. The curtains were drawn tightly. How could she be feeling this haunting, piercing stare?

Quietly Becky sat up in her bed moving her hand slowly to the corner of the curtain. Putting her face close to the glass, she seized the corner of the curtain between her fingers and began to pull it back. Peering into the still summer night she saw no one. Nothing moved outside her window. With a deep sigh of relief, she fell back into her pillow, relieved but perplexed by the sensation of being stalked.

She slept restlessly that night, yet with no reason for alarm. After all, she hadn't seen anything move. But what she hadn't seen was in the sand just below her window.

Footprints. Footprints much like those found by Eleanor Pippin on the Sanibel shore just a few days earlier.

CHAPTER 5

Earthquake

Even with Sanibel's resilience, and the optimistic attitudes of the residents, it had been a difficult year for this lush tropical resort island. Ten months earlier, hurricane Ellie had swept across the heart of the island with category four winds, leaving a path of devastation unprecedented in the history of Southwest Florida. While no lives were lost, the financial toll was staggering with immeasurable emotional consequences. The island was just beginning to recover from the piles of rubble and blue-tarped roofs when this visitation from an unknown invader came, bringing fear that even a hurricane did not evoke. That fear, cold and stark was about to be transformed to terror.

It was around 5:00 a.m. when a rumble shook the Island. In fact, it was 5:07 a.m. to be exact, because a total power failure swept across Sanibel like an evil hand of darkness. The earth shook, causing windows to crack, dishes to rattle and residents to leap out of their beds with a start.

"Mary, what was that!?" Tom shouted.

"I don't know. It felt like an earthquake...or some horrible explosion."

"Where's the radio hon? We've got to find out what's going on."

Mary retrieved the flashlight from the bedside drawer and sent a shaft of light around the room to find the small battery powered radio the Johnsons used during storms.

"There it is Tom. Up on the book shelf."

As Tom made his way to the bookshelves, the bedroom door flew open with a frightened Marty jumping in the bed with Mary.

"Momma, what was that noise? My bed shook!"

"We're not sure, sweetheart. Dad's going to turn on the radio to see if there is any news. Tom, I'm going to go with Marty and we're going to check the rest of the children."

"Okay, honey. I'll see what I can find out from the radio."

Mary and Marty made their way with the flashlight to the other end of the house where the children's rooms were located. Becky, Kristy and Ben were so exhausted from the stress of the day before that the rumble had not even roused them.

"Let's let them sleep, Marty. We'll wake them when we find out something."

"Okay Momma. What do you think it was? Do you think someone dropped a bomb on Sanibel?"

Mary held back a chuckle and said, "Oh no, honey. I don't think anyone dropped a bomb. I'm sure there is a very logical explanation."

The truth is, Marty was closer to the truth in her guess than anyone might expect. Breaking news reported that there had been an explosion on the Sanibel Causeway. Details were scarce, but there were rumors flying that one of the causeway bridges was gone.

Tom stayed near the radio hoping to get more information, while Mary and Marty fixed a pitcher of fresh orange juice.

"Momma, this all seems like a bad dream. I just want to wake up and find that none of these horrible things are true."

"Me too, honey. But it is not a dream. But I can assure you, sweetheart, that whatever all this is about God will see us through."

"I know, Mom. But I'm scared. I just want it all to be over."

At that moment Tom's cell phone rang.

"Hello."

"Tom, this is Pete. Have you heard the news?"

"I've heard bits and pieces. They're talking about an explosion on the causeway."

"That's right, Tom. I just got word that the two bridges closest to the island are gone. It seems someone used dynamite. Tom, they think it's another incident with our mysterious invaders."

"Pete, we've lost power…and the phone's dead too."

"That seems to be the case all across the island."

"Pete, does anyone have a clue of what's going on? Who are these people and what do they want?"

"No one knows much, Tom, but it seems that whoever we're up against has a plan…and they are incredibly crafty. I have a feeling we're going to find out who they are and what they want soon enough."

"So, Tom, are you going to go ahead and have church services this morning?"

"I think we should, Pete. People need to hear a word of hope. If nothing else, it will be good to get together just to pray."

"I agree Tom. Sara and I will come on up to the church around 8:00 a.m. ."

"Thanks Pete. We'll see you there. If you hear any more news before that, let me know."

"I'll keep you posted. See you soon Pastor. I'll be praying for you."

"We'll be praying for you and Sarah too…in fact, we'll be praying for all of Sanibel. May God help us."

The eastern sky began to reveal a dim glow of morning sun as dawn was approaching. With the light would come a new sense of hope.

"Mary, let's wake up the children and tell them what's happening. After we've had some time to talk and pray, I think we should drive down to Cypress Cove Beach and see what has happened to the causeway."

"Okay, Tom. I'll get them stirring."

As the Johnson family gathered in the living room, the sun was now fully above the horizon, casting shadowed light across the island. With the air conditioning out of commission for over an hour now, the summer heat and humidity were already beginning to infiltrate the home. Tom calmly explained to his four children the seriousness of the situation.

"Kids, we don't know who or what we are facing, but it's a critical situation. We must stay on the alert. The best thing we can do right now is to pray."

Each of the Johnson children offered up passionate prayers for protection, wisdom and guidance. Mary closed the time of prayer with words of thanksgiving. Mary had that wonderful ability to trust God…and believe that He would make good out of every situation.

"Kids, we're going to load up in the van and go down to Cypress Cove Beach. We can see the causeway from there and get some idea of just how serious things are." Tom explained.

Quietly and quickly the Johnsons made their way to the van. They had just enough time to drive down to the beach, and then get back to get ready for church services.

As the Johnsons approached the beach parking area, they noticed that several islanders had the same idea. There must have been over two hundred people gathered on the shore. Tom let the family out and parked the van several hundred yards away. Mary and the children waited for Tom so they could approach the shore together.

Like the other residents who had already gathered, the Johnson family stood in a hushed awe. Two huge cavities were ripped through the causeway, leaving it a series of disconnected islands, no longer attaching Sanibel to the mainland.

"Cut off." Someone muttered.

"Isolated to face this alone." One voice whispered.

Despair hung so thick in that morning air that you could feel it. It was a smothering, choking terror of the unknown—with an even greater fear of what might be next.

Tom broke the stillness with words of encouragement. "Folks, can I have your attention please? We're going to gather at the church at 10:00 o'clock to pray. Perhaps by then we'll have a better idea of what we're up against. Don't lose heart. We're going to be alright."

Tom had a lot of respect on Sanibel. Even people who did not agree with his evangelical theology had to admit he had a faith that was genuine. Tom loved the people of Sanibel, and they knew it. They found new hope and courage in his words—and many would show up later at Community Church to pray.

Ray of Hope

CHAPTER 6

Fear of the unknown is relentless. It opens the doors of speculation and imagination, which often magnify reality into a realm of panic and terror. It was precisely that kind of fear that was beginning to consume Sanibel Island. A dark cloud of merciless mystery hung heavy over the remaining isolated residents. Usually the light of truth shed upon those unknown fears brings relief, but what the islanders were about to learn would bring no comfort to them.

Mayor Todd had put in a call not only to Pastor Tom Johnson, but to the other pastors on the island as well. "We're calling a town meeting at noon at Periwinkle Park. The F.B.I. and some of our own police force have investigated the old freighter and we want to give a report. Could you make an announcement at your church services?"

"I'll be glad to, Mayor. We're praying for you Mayor Todd."

"Thanks, Pastor Tom. We all need that right now."

Ordinarily Community Church had three Sunday morning worship services, but today, they would have only one at 10:00 a.m. Frank, the church custodian, had made a makeshift sign to put out in front of the building that said:

Today
One Service Only
10:00 a.m.
COME PRAY!

Frank had also fired up the generator to provide enough electricity to provide some light and to have a few fans blowing.

As people began to gather in the beautiful old sanctuary, dimly lit, with fans providing a gentle breeze, they had a taste of nostalgic Community Church. There was no air conditioning, no spotlights flooding the chancel area...and no P.A. system to fill the sanctuary with artificial sound. It was simple and serene.

The service began with Ruth Neal, the church organist playing a powerful rendition of "How Great Thou Art," on the grand piano. Ruth had the uncanny ability to create sounds from that piano that made it seem as if the notes each had a life of its own. Her opening song blew out the clouds of despair and ushered in a wave of hope and new optimism.

Pastor Tom began with the words of the Apostle Paul: "Rejoice in the Lord always. Again, I say. Rejoice." After a short prayer, Tom called Burt Smith up to lead the congregation in some great hymns of faith. A spirit of confidence in Christ permeated the place. Tom didn't really preach—he simply shared some Scriptures about trust... and God's answer to fear. Then he called the people to a time of prayer.

Heartfelt prayers echoed throughout the building, but

probably the most touching of all was the prayer of eight year old Jonathan Rogers.

"Dear God," he said, "We know that you know everything that is going on. We love you and we trust you to take care of us. Please help us. Amen."

As the service concluded Tom announced about the city-wide gathering at Periwinkle Park. When he mentioned that a report was coming about the strange ship on the shore, a hush came over the people. There was a sense among the crowd that soon they would know what they were facing, and that they would need the faith and trust they had just experienced to sustain them through the days ahead.

CHAPTER 7

Fear

While the population on Sanibel Island is dramatically reduced during summer, still a huge crowd gathered at Periwinkle Park at noon. The majority of the people were year-round residents. Many tourists had left the island earlier with the report of the ship's landing. A trailer had been brought in with a portable P.A. system so that everyone could hear the report. The crowd quickly quieted as Mayor Todd made his way up on to the trailer.

"Citizens of Sanibel. Before I give the details of the F.B.I. report I want to call upon Pastor Tom Johnson to lead us in a time of prayer. Following the report, we will address any questions you might have. Ron Janes, from the office of the F.B.I. as well as Warren Davis, our own Chief of Police will help field your questions. Pastor Johnson, would you please lead us in prayer?"

Pastor Tom stepped up on to the trailer next to Mayor Todd, who handed him the microphone.

"Before I pray, I want to invite us all to take a moment for silent prayer to offer up to God our own concerns for family, friends and neighbors. Let's pray."

After more than a minute of silence, Tom Johnson

prayed for the people of Sanibel with a passion unlike anything they had heard before. His love and care for the entire community was evident in every word. Equally evident was his faith in God to provide and guide through the difficult times. At one point, Tom reached out and placed his hand on Mayor Todd's shoulder and said a special prayer for the mayor, as well as the police, firemen and other rescue workers. It was a prayer that set the tone for some grave news to be handled with hope.

"Thank you, Pastor Johnson for that prayer." The mayor gave Pastor Tom a gentle hug, demonstrating a sincere appreciation for Tom's care for the community.

The mayor began his remarks. "Ladies and gentlemen, we are faced with a very dangerous situation. Some time in the middle of the night last Thursday a freighter ship of unknown origin was found stranded upon our beaches. It became evident after preliminary investigation that someone was on board that ship and had made their way to a place of hiding on our island. After further research we have learned significant details that have prompted me to put the island under a state of emergency."

Gasps and whispers swept across the crowd.

"First of all, the ship seems to be a trade vessel of the French fleet. It appears that the crew, however, were not French merchants. With evidence of violence on board the ship, it is the conclusion of the F.B.I. that the ship was hijacked by some undetermined pirateers."

The mayor paused a moment collecting his thoughts and emotions for the most difficult news he yet must tell.

"Secondly, after contact with the French Government we have learned that the ship has been considered 'lost at sea' since last September, not returning to harbor after hurricane Ellie worked her way across the Atlantic

Ocean. By thorough investigation of conditions on the ship, as well as a study of footprints on the shore, it would suggest that as many as two hundred people disembarked on to our island. All or most of them were barefooted. Conditions would further suggest that they were dehydrated and malnourished."

The mayor paused…then continued.

"My friends, it is very clear that we are faced with a threat from a group of people who are both desperate and dangerous. On board we found evidence of violent crimes of torture and murder, as well as some signs pointing to cannibalism."

A gasp went through the crowd. Some began to sob. One woman fainted.

"Pardon me for being so graphic, but the stench of rotting flesh and the infestation of maggots made it extremely difficult for the officers to conduct their research. Whoever has come to our island has been living in those conditions for many days, which could lead to extreme mental and psychological dysfunction. That tells us that whoever is hiding on this island is dangerously unpredictable."

It was clear that Mayor Todd was having great difficulty in bringing this news to the people of Sanibel. Often he fought back tears.

"Events of the past two days further confirm our cause for alarm. We know that the intruders have secured weapons and are not restrained from using them. It is apparent that these individuals have some militia expertise, having set dynamite charges to the causeway bridges, isolating us from the mainland. We have yet to determine who they are or what they want. Today's events would lead us to believe that soon we will have a better idea regarding those issues."

Attempting to put the citizens of Sanibel at ease, Mayor Todd secured his composure and spoke with confidence.

"We are doing all we can to provide safety and security on the island. Please never go out alone and do not go out after dark at all. Keep all of your doors and windows locked. We are trying to arrange a ferry service for those who would like to evacuate the island. The Community Church and Ramey's Market are teaming up together to provide a central command post. Generators will be running there to provide air conditioning and meal preparation. Cots are being placed in all Christian education classrooms for those who prefer to stay in the guarded area of central command. Are there any questions?"

"Do you think these are terrorists?" A red-headed woman with a screechy voice shouted from the back of the crowd.

"We are considering that possibility. Al Qaeda has not been ruled out."

"Are you bringing in the National Guard to protect us?"

"Absolutely. A full division is on its way as we speak and will arrive by boat before dark this evening."

A man, red-faced and frustrated with the entire report shouted, "Should we get guns to protect ourselves?"

"I do not recommend that at all. We could easily fall into a panic here and develop a mob mentality if we do not be careful. Remember Pastor Tom's prayer. Let's be wise—and let's work together."

The mayor continued. "As I said, right now we are doing all we can to keep everyone safe. I suggest that either you secure yourself as best you can in your own home, or move on in to Central Command before night fall. Remember, the National Guard will be rolling in with plenty of help.

We will search the island and resolve this situation as soon as possible. Are there any further questions?"

Jack Barnes, manager of the Sea Dog Restaurant spoke up. "Yes, I have a question for Chief Davis. Many of us men are willing to help. Would you consider deputizing us so that we can assist in protecting our families and neighbors?"

"That's a great idea, Jack. Everyone who would like to volunteer to assist the police force meet me over at my squad car after we dismiss here. I'll have to screen all volunteers, but it will be a tremendous help to have many of you on the force."

Hazel Jones, owner of Hazel's Hair Boutique spoke up next. "How about some kitchen and cleaning crews up at Central command?" I'd be happy to work with Pastor Johnson's wife, Mary, to organize that."

"That's wonderful!" Mayor Todd pronounced.

"The ladies of the Catholic Guild will bring all of their quilts to help with the sleeping rooms at the church," offered Myra Rose Kinney, a devout Catholic from St. Isabel's.

"This is our Sanibel at its best," declared the Mayor. "We pulled together through the hurricane, and we will pull together through this."

Spirits were high. You could almost touch the optimism in the air. But that was not to last. Like a fog rolling in from some mysterious shore, a pall of dismay fell over the crowd. In the distance they heard a siren. A siren that grew louder and closer with every pounding heart beat. It was as if everyone knew this was no ordinary emergency run. It meant something new had unfolded in their nightmare.

The screaming patrol car pulled in among the throng of people. Officer Schmidt jumped out of the car and ran directly to the platform to speak with Chief Davis and Mayor Todd. Forgetting that he still held the microphone Mayor Todd uttered words that he had no intention for the crowd to hear.

"Oh no! They have hostages!"

CHAPTER 8

Hostages

It's hard to imagine that anyone could be on Sanibel or Captiva Island and not be aware of the horrifying drama that had been unfolding in recent days. Cindy Gray, a young conservation intern from New York State, however, had no idea the islands were in danger.

Cindy had come to spend the summer doing research on Sanibel and Captiva, determining long range effects of hurricane Ellie on the wildlife of the islands. A wealthy couple from New York City had provided Cindy housing, allowing her to say in their luxurious condominium on Captiva Island.

On Saturday afternoon Cindy had gone to Fort Myers airport to pick up seven fifth grade girls who would spend all day Sunday exploring the Ding Darling nature preserve. Partly because the condominium was a long way from the causeway explosion—and mostly because the girls had stayed up until 2:00 a.m. playing games, no one heard the rumble, nor felt the tremor from the blast. Although the girls woke up reluctantly that morning, they were full of anticipation for the explorations of the day. After breakfast, Cindy, along with these seven enthusiastic fifth grade girls, headed out on a hiking adventure they would never forget.

The hikers had just passed the entry gate and taken the turn off of the paved road onto the dirt path when they heard rustling sounds in the dense brush. Thinking it must be birds, the girls were not alarmed, but curious to see what beautiful creatures might be just beyond view. Soon their curiosity turned to concern as they began to hear the sound of splashing, like something violently thrashing in the shallow wetlands. Above the sound of the turbulent water they heard voices. Voices that were unfamiliar and urgent. It quickly became clear that the sound was that of someone running through the shallow waters, quickly approaching where Cindy and the girls stood.

Bursting from the heavy underbrush came a cluster of men; gaunt, black men manifesting what seemed like demonic expressions and sounds. The girls screamed at the sight of their attackers, but there was no one to hear. Everyone else was enamored with the terrifying mystery that gripped Sanibel Island, so this Sunday morning, Ding Darling preserve was inhabited only by the beautiful creatures of paradise, eight terrified hikers and a band of desperate, violent men.

Quickly, the men surrounded Cindy and the fifth graders. They bound the girls' hands and covered their mouths with duct tape the men had acquired in one of their night time raids. Once each victim was secure, two of the men would pick her up and head northwest back into the shallow waters and deep brush. The girls were too terrified to even think about what was really happening, or where their adductors were taking them. They only wondered if they would get out of this situation alive.

Among the crowd of people gathered a Periwinkle Park

a whispered echo surged through the crowd: "Hostages?" While Mayor Todd never intended for everyone to hear, the truth is it would only have been a matter of time before the whole island would be buzzing with the news. Mayor Todd called the crowd to attention.

"Quiet, please everyone. The purpose of this meeting was to give you every bit of information we have so that we will all know what we are facing. In consultation with the F.B.I. and our own police Chief we feel that it is the best interest of everyone that Officer Schmidt give a detailed report to this gathering regarding a hostage situation that has developed within the last few hours.

The crowd applauded with approval. One of the reasons Mayor Todd was in his third term as mayor was because of his sense of openness and fairness. He respected and trusted the citizens of Sanibel, and because of that, they had the same trust and respect for him.

"Officer Schmidt. Please come and tell everyone just how much you know about the situation right now." Mayor Todd gestured to Officer Schmidt to step up to the microphone.

Officer Schmidt was obviously shaken by the whole situation. His voice was trembling as he related to the crowd that the lives of seven young girls and one adult sponsor were in grave danger.

"I was making security checks all around the Island with the Sanibel School on my list of rounds this morning. I pulled into the parking lot and immediately sensed something was wrong. It was so quiet—so somber. As I walked around to the back of the cafeteria I spotted a pile of garbage. I wondered where it had come from since school was not in session. As I drew closer, the stench was almost more than I could bear. Obviously the debris had been accumulating there for a few days and with the summer heat it quickly had become rancid.

After I had rounded the corner, near the back door of the cafeteria, I thought I saw a shadow. It moved so quickly, I wasn't sure, but there was a very clear sense that I was not alone. Just as I put my hand to the knob of the back door, I heard a tap on the window coming from the second story classrooms. As I turned my gaze to the upstairs windows, a chill touched my very soul. There stood seven young girls and one woman, tied, gagged and blindfolded. Each girl was in the grip of two thin black men. The men were armed with guns and knives. As I peered in shock at the nightmarish scene, one man who clearly was a leader held up a sign that said:

WE TALK
BRING LEADER.
ONE MAN ONLY

"I think Police Chief Davis should tell you the rest."

Chief Davis replaced Officer Schmidt at the podium. "We don't know who the girls are, but we are doing all we can to collect information. We have asked the F.B.I. to designate one man to be a negotiator to discover who these people are and what they want."

Mayor Todd stepped up to the microphone. "Ladies and gentleman. It is clear that this is a very dangerous situation. I suggest that if you feel you must be going about the island, that you stay together in small groups. I recommend that as many of you who can move on in quickly at command headquarters at Community Church. We will post guards around that area to keep everyone safe. We are setting up tents and cots for further shelter. This is a time we must find strength in working and staying together."

While everyone was fearful, there remained an attitude of optimism. The people of Sanibel had pulled together through difficult times before, and they could do it again.

"Before we dismiss this gathering and all move to places of safety, I think it would be good for us to join hands and pray. Father Joseph, would you please come and lead us in a time of prayer?"

Father Joseph, like Tom Johnson, was also greatly respected on Sanibel. He'd been at St. Isabel's for nearly twenty years. He prayed,

> "Lord, you are the Shepherd who keeps watch over His sheep—and we know that you don't want to see even one little lamb get lost. O merciful God, help these children and their sponsor to be set free without harm. Please give wisdom to the F.B.I. agents, our Mayor and police force as they seek a solution for this tragedy of events. As you lay down your life for your sheep, help us to lay down our lives for one another, working in unity until peace is restored to Sanibel. We pray this is the Name of the Father, the Son and the Holy Spirit. Amen"

Little did Father Joseph realize, but his prayer had birthed an idea in his colleague, Tom Johnson. As soon as the Father made his way off of the platform, Pastor Tom pulled him aside and said, "Father Joseph. We need to talk. Can I meet you at St. Isabel's in about an hour?"

The Shepherds

Father Joseph had no idea what Tom Johnson had in mind when Tom called their secret meeting, but he had learned to trust Tom. They were not only colleagues in ministry, they had become friends. Tom and Father Joseph had served together on the Sanibel Community Action Team, (S.C.A.T.) that fought hard for a teen rec center at Periwinkle Park. Even though Sanibel was a resort-retirement island, it also was the home of dozens of children and teens.

It was about 4:00 p.m. as Father Joseph made his way from the church manse to the ornate sanctuary of St. Isabel's. Much to his surprise, Tom Johnson was not alone. Alan Kelso, pastor of the Congregational Church, Father Bill Kline, of the Episcopal Church and Rabbi Hinman of the Jewish congregation were there. Only Tom Johnson knew the reason for the special gathering.

Tom spoke first. "Men, our island is under siege. Our people are full of fear and despair. I believe we can help."

"What to you have in mind, Tom?" Asked Father Bill.

"Father Joseph's prayer today gave me an idea."

"My prayer? What was it about the prayer that has brought us together?"

"It was when you spoke of laying our lives down for one another."

"Now wait a minute Tom. Let's not get too literal about this." Alan Kelso spoke these words with a smile, for he and Tom had had many discussions about how to interpret Scripture.

"I'll be honest with you men. It might mean that we are literally laying our lives down." Tom said calmly.

"What do you mean, Tom?" Rabbi Hinman said softly.

"Gentlemen. Seven young girls and their sponsor are in the hands of treacherous men. These men have proven themselves to be heartless and cruel."

"That certainly is true," interrupted Pastor Kelso. The others nodded in agreement.

"What are you thinking, Tom?" asked Father Joseph.

"I'm thinking an exchange."

"Exchange? You mean an exchange of hostages?" Inquired Pastor Kelso.

"Yes." Tom said simply.

"Who do you have in mind?" Rabbi Hinman asked reluctantly.

"Us. I am suggesting we offer ourselves as an exchange for the girls."

Father Bill protested. "Tom, you can't do that! You have a young family of your own. They might kill …"

Tom interrupted. "I know they might kill us. I also know that they might torture and kill those little girls."

"I agree with Tom," declared Pastor Kelso, "far better that our lives be on the line rather than the lives of those children."

"Please understand, brothers. You must pray and search

your own heart about doing this. We will fully understand if anyone does not want to be involved." Tom was so gracious in his remarks. He didn't want anyone making a decision under compulsion. It was going to be a monumental task, one in which only those fully committed would be able to endure.

"I'm in!" said Father Joseph.

"Me too!" declared Pastor Kelso.

"I'll do it!" Rabbi Hinman spoke the words firmly, with passion.

"May God help us," pronounced Father Bill, as he put his hands firmly on the shoulders of the men gathered around him.

"Then it is settled. I'll call Chief Davis right away and we'll see how soon we can make this happen. Time is critical."

With spiritual resolve and compassionate conviction, the men joined hands as if preparing for battle. Pastor Kelso prayed fervently for the wisdom and grace of God to abound in their endeavor. They would reconvene as soon as Tom got things arranged with Chief Davis. The shepherds of Sanibel were laying down their lives for the sheep.

As these men of God were preparing for a great spiritual battle, the National Guard was gathering on the only remaining connected island of the Sanibel causeway for another battle.

CHAPTER 10

Helicopters

Because of the war on terror, with troops in Iraq and Afghanistan, National Guard forces were depleted. On this Sunday evening they could only muster about fifty soldiers; men and women ready to bravely protect the people of Sanibel.

P.T. Boats that transported about twenty each were launched from the peninsula of the crumbled causeway, hastily heading toward the shores of Sanibel. As the first P.T. boat drew near to the island, shots rang out.

"Snipers to our right, Captain!" shouted one of the soldiers.

A man was hit. Blood oozed from his left shoulder as he writhed in pain. A second man was down...this wound was to the abdomen. For fear of stray bullets harming residents of Sanibel, the captain ordered the soldiers to hold their fire.

"Turn it hard, soldier!" Barked the captain. "We've got to land at another point."

The boat made a hard left turn with the two other craft following suit.

"Let's go on around past the light house and approach from the other side."

Quickly the boats rounded the point and broke out into the gulf side of Sanibel. The sun set was as beautiful as the thousands of serene sunsets Sanibel had seen before, but there was nothing placid about this sunset. In fact, the prospect of darkness coming to Sanibel before the troops could land was unthinkable.

"Head the boats in there." The captain pointed to an area that seemed most likely to get them close to shore. The shallow waters, made more so by low tide made it impossible for the boats to get fully to shore. They would be forced to run aground and then make their way through the water to the beach.

Once again the sound of gunfire pierced the air, and still another soldier fell wounded. A young woman who had been in the guard less than a year pressed her hand firmly to her right thigh as the stain of blood marched mercilessly down her leg.

"Medic! Get to this soldier and get that bleeding stopped!"

It was clear the other boats were suffering casualties. It was as if a swarm of hornets were surrounding the soldiers, stinging them with deadly force.

"We've got to get out of here. Let's return to base and regroup. We don't know how or where to predict a safe landing.

Reluctantly the P.T. Boats distanced themselves from the deadly shore and returned to the launching area. As soon as the ships arrived, the event Commander sent two Apache helicopters to attempt a support landing on the island.

As the helicopters approached, they too encountered gun fire from the ground. This was one of those winless battles with the inability to defend themselves due to the potential of harming residents on the Island.

"We've got to regroup. They can't have gunmen everywhere.

We'll find their point of weakness and then we will make our move." The commander called the helicopters back to base.

"Tomorrow. First light. We will try again. But tonight, Sanibel must face its foe alone.

CHAPTER 11

Negotiations

The gunfire was heard all across the island. Panic and fear filled the hearts of the people as they made their way to Command Central at Community Church and Ramey's Market. It seemed as if no one had decided to go it alone in their own home. The whole town was there.

By now, Chief Davis had deputized about forty residents. Along with his police force, fire department and city employees, all now armed and ready to protect the citizens of Sanibel, a force of nearly a hundred surrounded the compound. Tiki torches had been placed about twenty feet apart, the full circumference of the area. Even though fear touched the heart and mind of every soul, there was a sense of safety in being together…in coming together as community to protect one another.

As the sun set fully on Sanibel, a darkness engulfed the island with a stifling heaviness. The last of the residents had made their way into the compound and folks were settling in for a long, sleepless night. As the last vehicle pulled into the crowded parking lot, a city van pulled out. In that van rode eight brave men; Mayor Todd, Chief Davis, F.B.I. Agent Ron Janes and five dedicated pastors hoping to negotiate with a band of insane terrorists barricaded securely at the Sanibel School.

The note from the invaders was clear. Only one man was to approach them. That one man must have the authority to speak for the people. Mayor Todd had immediately volunteered to be that man.

At first, Agent Janes had protested. "No, let me do it," he said. "I've had experience in negotiations."

"I know you have, Ron, but can you speak for the people of Sanibel?"

Chief Davis spoke in support of the mayor. "Mayor Todd is right, Ron. Our own people trust him, and that means a lot for the citizens."

"It's not our protocol," the agent spoke with reluctance. "But I do understand. It is agreed then. Mayor Todd will be the point man."

When the van arrived at the Sanibel School a microphone was placed upon the mayor so that the conversations could be heard in the van which would be parked about a half of a mile from the school. As he walked alone toward the enemy's fortress, Mayor Todd was demonstrating his love for the people of Sanibel, as well as his dedication as a public servant. Within a hundred yards of the middle school, two armed men joined the mayor escorting him to the point of negotiations.

In the van, the men listened intently to the radio for any report. A whisper came as Mayor Todd spoke into the microphone. "I can see the leader. He is about fifty feet away. Tell those pastors to pray!"

The pastors were praying. It seemed as if the only hope at this point would involve some sort of miracle.

"Halt!" A sharp command rang through the radio. "State your name and position!"

"My name is Frank Todd. I am the Mayor of Sanibel."

The leader of the murderous mob looked intently into the mayor's eyes. "Do you speak for the people who dwell here?"

"I do."

Mayor Todd was impressed with the leader's accomplished grasp of the English language. It was evident that this man was the only one who spoke English fluently. The others seemed to be straining to comprehend the conversation.

In a dialect the Mayor did not recognize, the leader seemed to be explaining to the men around him what was happening.

In the van, Agent Janes turned on a tape recorder. "This will help us determine who these people are. It's not a language I recognize, but I know they will be able to sort it out at the lab."

"We want food, water, and medical supplies." The leader said firmly. "We want no soldiers to come to this island or the girls will die. Bring the supplies tomorrow before noon, and we will talk more."

"We will meet your requests." Mayor Todd replied.

"If you meet all of our demands no one will die. If you attempt to attack, the bloodshed will be much."

"I understand." Mayor Todd gulped and spoke further. "Sir, May I make a request?"

"What is your request?"

"A hostage exchange sir. Five leaders of our community have offered to take the place of the girls."

"Five men for little girls. I think the little girls are more strategic for our cause."

The mayor knew that the leader was right. The motivation to protect the lives of these innocent young girls would be higher. Knowing this, the Mayor spoke persuasively.

"Sir, these men are leaders. They are men with families. They would be an irreplaceable loss to our community. I can assure you that the community will be equally constrained to meet your demands to save the lives of these men."

In the van, the five pastors huddled in quiet prayer that this tyrant would possess even the smallest amount of mercy to make the exchange.

"Very well. I will exchange."

The men almost shouted in the van. The mayor gave an expression of deep gratitude. "Oh, thank you, sir. The five men are in a van about a half of a mile away. I will bring them here."

"I will bring out the girls."

This was the first test of trust. This exchange would set the course for future negotiations. If this went smoothly, there would be hope for future resolution.

Mayor Todd made his way with armed escort back to the van.

When they arrived at the van, the five pastors climbed out with their arms raised high in the universal sign of surrender. The gunman motioned to the men to begin their march to the exchange point.

At that moment, the back door of the van burst open. The gunmen turned with startled faces, cocking their guns, ready to squelch this disruption.

"Dad! Dad! Let me go with you. I want to help save those girls!"

"Ben, you should have stayed at the compound!"

Quickly the gunmen responded by rounding up all of the hostages. The stakes were higher now. The exchange would be for five men and a teenage boy.

CHAPTER 12

The Fortress

Even though Ben's impulsiveness to be involved in the exchange had complicated negotiations, the terrorists remained true to their commitment to release the girls. Seven trembling girls stood in the hot and humid summer night air. With hands bound, they were unable to swat the attacking mosquitoes that were aggressively biting at their young flesh. But where was the young woman who was the leader of the girls?

Unfortunately, in his negotiations, Mayor Todd had only mentioned the girls. Of course, he meant the entire group when he presented his terms to the leader, but seizing on the mayor's omission, the leader gave the negotiations a turn that kept them strongly in his favor. Now he had five community leaders, a young man, as well as the young woman. His position of leverage had not been weakened.

Quickly, the sinister dark captors bound the hands of the men and boy, covering their mouths with duct tape. The hostages were then moved quietly into the enemies' fortress as human collateral for the demands that were yet to come.

Sanibel Middle School hardly resembled a school

any more. Desks had been stacked along the windows to serve as shields for battle. Each class room was strewn with ransacked furniture, disheveled books and papers. A building once filled with laughter and learning had become a house of torture and terror.

Perhaps more disturbing than the scattered debris was the oppressive odor. Ben recognized it at once to be the same smell he encountered on the bike path last Thursday night. With the clutter, the heat, the aggravating mosquitoes—compounded with the nauseous smell, it was almost more than anyone could bear. How could those little girls have endured such torment? Had the terror driven them mad? Would they be scarred for a lifetime for the horror of the past twelve hours?

As they made their way slowly through the dark halls, they noticed that there were at least two men stationed at each window. Each one had at least one gun, many had two. Strapped to their side or lying near them was one of the large butcher knives from Community Church. It's hard to imagine these instruments that had served to foster fellowship and friendship were now weapons to fill hearts with fear. Tom tried to get some idea of a count, but with the darkness, it was hard to determine just how many men were in the school. He was sure there were no less than one hundred.

The captives were led through the gym to the windowless men's locker room. A candle in the corner of the room cast mysterious shadows. Through the dim light, Tom peered hoping to see the young woman alive and unharmed. She was not in the room. They were keeping her somewhere else. He could not imagine what it must be like for her in some horrid solitary confinement. Tom offered up a silent prayer in her behalf.

The locker room was equipped with benches that were bolted to the painted concrete floor. Each captive was strapped to his own bench, securely separated from each other and utterly defenseless. With the locker rooms serving as hurricane shelter areas they were nearly impregnable by outside forces. They served as the perfect prison for the hostages.

As Tom lay there in the silence in the still, dim room his thoughts were full of his son, Ben. How could he do this? Why did he do it? He was safe in the compound. It was at this point that Tom was overwhelmed with emotions. "I was willing to give my life for the girls—for the people of Sanibel—but now, they have my son. My only son." As those words made their way through his weary brain he could not help but think of the cross.

"It's one thing to give up one's own life. It is another to give up the life of one's child." At that moment Tom Johnson, who had preached hundreds of sermons, spoken countless times of God's love was overwhelmed by the love of God. "That's exactly what He did. He willingly, lovingly gave up the life of His own son so that I could go free—just like those girls." Tom began to sob. The others thought his tears were tears of despair, but they were not. Each drop that streamed down the pastor's face was a droplet of gratitude. Somehow, overwhelmed by the compassion—and yes, the very presence of God, Tom Johnson was filled with hope. The suffering of the cross meant redemption...reconciliation...and Tom was confident those elements were in the works again.

Ben was having thoughts of his own as he lay strapped to the bolted bench. "I know Dad understands. He knows we think alike. I couldn't stay there in the compound and do nothing." Deep down Ben knew his dad was proud of him, but he also was aware that if they got out of this alive, he would probably be grounded from all electronics for one year.

While Pastor Tom and his son, Ben, were reflecting on the last hour, Rabbi Hinman was also pondering the developments of the exchange. As he lay strapped to the hard locker room bench his thoughts kept returning to the altar of sacrifice. He had read the words of Passover hundreds of times, and much like Pastor Tom, had a new revelation of the sacrificial lamb in this encounter.

What he could not comprehend was why the boy had done what he did. *That stupid boy....* He thought. *Probably in for some thrill—or trying to impress some girl.* But deep down, Rabbi Hinman knew better. Gazing upon the boy, stretched out on the locker room altar, Rabbi Hinman kept thinking of Abraham...and in the boy, he saw young Isaac.

It was a time for reflection for each of the men. On this threshold of death, each was taking inventory of all that he believed...of all they had taught and preached. Truth that is tested has a purity about it...like fine gold.

On that endless hot summer night, five men and a youth lay silently, each strapped to his own altar, thinking...praying...hoping for some divine intervention to come. As each drifted off to sleep, Ben got the attention of his dad by snapping his fingers. Through the shadowy light, Tom could see his son's right hand. With keen precision Ben signed the phrase, "I love you." Tom signed back, "I love you."

CHAPTER 13

Command Central

Nothing was typical about this Monday morning on Sanibel. Even in summer, when the snowbirds have gone home to the North, the island would normally be bustling with activity. Folks from the mainland filled the specialty shops as well as the beaches even on the warmest summer days. Vacationing young families took advantage of the warm gulf waters. But on *this* Monday on Sanibel, there was almost no traffic. The shops were closed. In many ways the island seemed like a ghost town.

While most of the island was engulfed in the oppressive silence, there was an abundance of activity at what had become the community command post. With generators running at full throttle, Ramey's Market and Community Church were providing relief from the heat, food and water, and protection from the invaders. Tents were strewn across the lawns with dozens of cots in each one. Many residents had brought their own tents, making the compound look much like a refugee camp.

The night before, about 10:00 p.m. Mayor Todd, Chief

Davis and Agent Janes had returned with the seven frightened girls. The girls were now in a doctor's care in one of the upstairs classrooms of the education wing. Other than minor dehydration, the girls had suffered no physical harm. Time would tell the depth of their emotional wounds. At least they were talking now, which was therapeutic in itself. Everyone was relieved that the girls were safe.

While Mary Johnson was happy for the release of the young girls, she was distraught over her son. Tom had confided in her of his plan for the exchange, but there was no mention of Ben being included in that exchange. Was that Tom's idea—or had something simply gone wrong? While she was perplexed about how it all came about, her greater concern was how it would all turn out.

Mayor Todd had called for another town meeting. He knew he needed to report to the people of the demands of the invaders. At 11:00 a.m. the people gathered in the middle of Command Central for a full report.

"As you all know," the Mayor began, "the seven girls have been released."

At that remark applause filled the air.

"I know that most of you are aware that to secure their release we made a hostage exchange. The terrorists now hold Father Joseph, Father Bill Kline, Rabbi Hinman, Pastor Alan Kelso, Pastor Tom Johnson."...then he paused ..." And Tom's son, Ben."

Hearing that news for the first time, some gasped.

The mayor went on. "They continue to hold hostage the young woman, Cindy Gray, whom we have learned to be an intern environmentalist who was stationed on Captiva Island. Last night, we talked briefly with the leader of this dangerous enemy, who presented modest demands, but who has further requests to be presented later today. At this point they are simply requesting food, water and medical supplies. A shipment of those items will be delivered after this meeting. They furthermore asked for our assurance that no soldiers would be dispensed to the Island. The National Guard has been directed to remain in readiness at their encampment on the mainland."

Someone shouted, "So, the National Guard is not coming to protect us!?"

"That's right. Not for now. We will negotiate as long as we can, and to the extent that we can with peaceful measures without compromising the safety of our citizens."

"Sounds like you've already compromised our safety!" Exclaimed an angry woman in the middle of the crowd.

"The leader promised us that no one would be harmed as long as we cooperate. We must give that commitment a chance to see us through this crisis to a point of reconciliation. I assure you that if at any point there is a betrayal of their promises, we will take aggressive steps to defend ourselves. We must be patient and play this thing out as far as we can with as little harm done as possible."

While the situation continued to be grim, the crowd did find some sense of hope—some evidence of progress in the mayor's report. Mostly because of their trust, and partly because of desperation, the citizens were willing to allow the negotiations to take their course.

Following the town meeting everyone returned to the task of transforming Community Church into a defensible fortress. The historic chapel had been restructured to appear more like a military hospital. The men had boarded up all of the windows. The pews had been placed outside in shady areas to provide gathering places for rest. In place of the pews, cots had been brought in for those who were ill or suffering from the heat. The generators were unable to provide air conditioning for all of the facilities, but the old sanctuary was one area that was being kept cool.

The fellowship hall, air-conditioned as well, was now the dining hall. Hundreds of meals were served daily by the efficient crew led by Mary Johnson and Hazel Jones. At night the elderly and families with very young children were brought into the large cool room to sleep on mats on the floor.

While the work progressed steadily at the church, Ramey's Store was also being remodeled. The parking garage was lined with tents and cots, having become a community of refugees. It provided cover from the hot sun, as well as protection from the afternoon rains. Cars had been parallel parked fully around the parameter of the garage with armed men stationed strategically to provide protection. Each man served a twelve hour shift, rotating in such a way that the make-shift village was under constant surveillance.

The windows of Ramey's market and restaurant had been boarded up. Entrances into the store were restricted. With the city under a state of emergency, food and water supplies must be rationed and protected. Normal sales had been brought to a halt with the Mayor's declaration. While some residents complained, most understood the need to control supplies.

Little did Becky Johnson know that her summer mission trip this year would be to her own neighbors and friends. Instead of rebuilding a school and ministering to children in Jamaica, she found herself coordinating children's activities on her own Island of Sanibel.

Becky's younger sister, Kris, also had a gift for working with children. She had that special touch to make a child smile…or even laugh out loud. The two of them worked smoothly as a team, leading in games, songs and other activities so that the parents could concentrate on reinforcing Central Command. Besides providing much needed childcare, it was obvious the activities were helping the children to cope with the stress of their dilemma.

Marty, even though she was only twelve got into the act of helping with the children also. She had written a play and was busily assigning parts and beginning rehearsals. Marty's friend, Anna, had written a couple of songs to go with the play, so now it had become a full blown musical. They called it, *Victory on Sanibel*. This original musical would serve as a pleasant distraction for all of the folks gathered in the compound.

All afternoon, the townspeople worked to protect themselves from their unknown foe. The strength of Sanibel was demonstrated in a constant spirit of cooperation. By nightfall, there would be a settling in…a sense of security and satisfaction. Yet, in spite of all of their labors, there remained an element of fear. Were there eyes peering at them through the darkness? Would the enemy strike in the night when their guard was down? Later, as they would make their way to cots and mats all across the compound attempting to get some sleep, no real rest would be found.

A Friend

The locker room at the Sanibel School was oppressive. With the stale, humid air, the stench from the guards was intensified, causing Ben to feel dizzy and nauseous. He wondered what time it was—or even what day it was. With no windows, it was impossible to discern the difference between night and day.

A gaunt black man carrying a 4–10 shot gun came into the dim room barking out orders to the guards. Quickly they hurried out of the room, leaving the hostages alone. Ben thought it unusual that they would be left alone in their prison cell. Something must be happening outside. Was the city meeting the demands of the invaders, or was there some kind of attack being launched to save them? The teen's imagination ran wild.

It was at that moment the door to the locker room opened slowly and silently. A small dark figure peered into the room with wide eyes, curiously surveying the situation. *That looks like a boy*...Ben thought. It was a boy. He looked to be about twelve. It was hard to guess since he was so thin...so small.

The boy crept into the room observing the hostages as

if they were an assortment of zoo animals on display. He paused for the longest time right in front of Ben. Slowly the boy drew very close and knelt by the bench where Ben was securely tied.

"If I remove the tape, do you promise not to yell?

Ben, like all of the rest in the room, was shocked to hear the boy speak English.

Ben nodded.

Gently, carefully the young boy removed the stifling duct tape from Ben's mouth. Ben took in several deep breaths before he spoke.

"You know English. Who are you? Who are these evil men? What do you wa…?"

The boy interrupted. "Shhhhhhhhh! Too many questions. They will be back soon. You are in great danger and I want to try to help you." The boy continued softly. "My name is Hadid. I am from Haiti, just like these other men. I learned English in the orphanage from an American missionary named Elizabeth. She was a special friend to me. Elizabeth died in the hurricane."

Ben spoke tenderly. "I'm sorry."

"Elizabeth not only taught me English. She told me about Jesus. She also told me that there were many Christians in America who care about the poor and suffering. She said they had plenty to share."

The boy was quiet for a moment. Ben wasn't sure if Hadid were listening for footsteps or collecting his thoughts. The boy continued.

"These desperate men have been hiding from the Haitian government. They overheard Elizabeth talking about the wealth in America. The waves of the hurricane had forced an old freighter ship to seek a port on Haiti. When the sailors abandoned their ship, these men boarded it and stole it in the night. I too longed for America, so I snuck on board as well."

Footsteps. The men were returning. Quickly Hadid put the duct tape back just as it had been. He rose and started toward the door. Two men burst into the room, shouting angry words at the boy. One struck him across the side of his face and shouted a command. Respectfully, Hadid submitted to their orders and left the room.

As Tom Johnson pondered the scene that had just unfolded before his eyes, and reflected on the words of the young Haitian boy, he was confident that God had placed a minister of hope in their midst. Tom immediately began to pray for Hadid.

Ben Johnson was praying also. He was grateful Hadid had come to him. Somehow he felt as if he had a new friend. There was a sense of hopefulness in Ben's heart that this friendship would somehow lead to their release. Hadid was brave—and he was kind. Ben knew the boy would be back.

For the first time since the six hostages had been strapped to the benches in that steamy locker room, the men sensed a lifting of their hopeless despair. Even though they were weak, having had nothing to eat or drink, they felt nourished by the prospect of their tortures end.

It was in that moment that the stillness was broken by a woman's scream. From another cell, not too far away, a young woman who had been kept in the terror of aloneness was in grave danger. All that could be heard was the shuffling of feet, the shout of an angry command...and then one last piercing scream.

Demands

As the truck pulled up to the drop point to unload the food, water and medical supplies that the terrorist leader had demanded, Chief Davis noticed the young woman held firmly in the grip of two armed captors.

"Oh no!" Exclaimed the chief. "That's Cindy Gray, the young internist. I think we are in for some more negotiations, but I fear that this time the stakes will be higher.

Chief Davis was right. The Haitian rebel leader knew that Cindy was his most prized possession. With arrogant assurance, the leader called for Mayor Todd to come forward to talk.

Bravely the Mayor made his way out of the truck and approached the ruthless rebel commander. "What do you want?" the mayor asked. "We have met all of your demands so far—and we are prepared to work with you as long as no one is harmed."

"Shut up!" The Commander shouted. "I am in charge of this conversation!"

It was at that moment that Mayor Todd remembered the report from the F.B.I.

Anyone living in these conditions would be unpredictably

dangerous, prone to emotional and psychological dysfunction.
The mayor had a brutal reminder of the kind of man with whom he was dealing.

"Yes sir." The mayor spoke respectfully. "Please forgive me, sir."

"That's better. Now. Here is what I want. First of all, I want someone more important than you to come talk to me. In your country you call them governors. I want your governor to come talk to me before the sun sets tomorrow."

"But ..." the mayor began, but caught himself.

The angry leader continued, ignoring the mayor's interruption. "Second, I want more guns. Big guns. Twenty-five machine guns and twenty-five grenade launchers. Bring those when the governor comes."

The vicious commander seemed to be carefully considering his next demand. It seemed as if he were tabulating something in his mind. "Ten million dollars. I want ten million dollars. Answer my demands before the sun sets tomorrow night or the girl dies."

The mayor took a risk. "But sir. That is less than thirty-six hours. As you know, we are cut off from the mainland. It will take time to meet these demands."

With a sly grin the Haitian leader responded. "Very well. I will give you five days before the girl dies." Then he laughed—a sinister laugh like that of some demon from the darkest pit. . "But at sunset tomorrow the torture will begin, so I suggest you work quickly."

Shaken, yet keeping unusual composure, the mayor replied. "We will work as quickly as possible. Please have mercy on us."

"Mercy? Mercy like me and my men have endured on

Haiti. Mercy like we have tasted on the relentless sea facing starvation and disease. Oh yes, we will give you mercy."

"Sir, tell me please." The mayor went on. "What is it you really want? Perhaps we can settle all of this sooner if you'll just tell us what you want."

"That, my friend, I will tell to your governor. Now go! Listen for the screams as the sun sets tomorrow night if my demands are not met."

The mayor walked quickly back to the waiting truck. "Warren, I know you heard the whole conversation. It's worse than we thought. I was so hopeful when we talked with them last night. He seemed reasonable."

Agent Janes interjected. "It only confirms the report. We are dealing with a violent, unpredictable enemy."

"That's what I feared, Ron. Let's keep this to ourselves until I've spoken to the governor. Our people have endured so much already," the mayor said compassionately.

"That's wise, Mayor. Well, at least we learned something."

"What's that, Ron?" Asked Chief Davis.

"They're Haitian. That's going to help us put some puzzle pieces together. Go ahead and call the governor, mayor. I'm going to put in a call to Port au Prince and speak to the consulate there."

"We've got to work fast." Mayor Todd spoke with urgency. "What do we do about the weapons Ron?"

"I'll work on that end of things too. I think I have an idea."

The three men drove hastily back to Command Central. They knew the citizens of Sanibel would want a report...in fact, they would expect one. Mayor Todd, who was always candid with the people he served knew there was a time when too much information could do more harm than good. He would simply tell the people that negotiations are continuing and that no one has been harmed...and that the governor is on his way.

Mayor Todd, Agent Ron Janes, and Chief Warren Davis spent the afternoon making calls to coordinate a response to the terrorists' demands. The mayor learned that the governor was on a special assignment by request of the president. He and seven other governors were visiting U.S. troops in Iraq to bring encouragement and to demonstrate confidence that the country had become more secure. The mayor was told that the earliest date he could possibly return would be Friday. The torture would begin at sunset on Tuesday.

With that news the three men looked at each other with dismay. "God help them," whispered Chief Davis.

"Is there nothing we can do, Ron? Can you persuade the president to let our governor come home?" The mayor pleaded.

"I'll do what I can, but I'm doubtful. It could appear to the insurgents in Iraq that the governor departed because of fear. The situation is still so tenuous there."

"I understand, Ron, but please try."

"I will."

Agent Ron Janes left the room to make more calls. At the same time, he was waiting to hear from the Haitian Consulate. Warren Davis was working on the guns and grenade launchers. Agent Janes had mentioned some sort of an idea—or plan, yet he had directed the police Chief to secure the weapons and have them in readiness on the mainland shore for delivery to Sanibel. All afternoon the men labored diligently to prepare their response.

After dinner, just as the sun was setting, people began to gather for the children's musical. Torches lighted the makeshift stage in front of the Christian Education building. The audience sat in lawn chairs or on blankets on the ground coming to support the children as well as have a chance to release some of the tension of their nightmare.

The musical was outstanding. Marty had developed a story about a small town that was being attacked by aliens from the planet Zoeton. The aliens were in costumes that made them look something like the Pillsbury Doughboy, bringing a smile to all of the spectators. In order to overcome the aliens, the town's people had to join hands and sing a song of hope and love. The children sang with confidence and courage:

> *Together we can face the danger.*
> *Together we can win.*
> *With love and unity we can stand together.*
> *Together we can win.*

After the aliens melted on the stage from the show of unity and courage, the crowd cheered. For the grand finale, Marty had everyone stand and sing:

> *Together we can face the danger.*
> *Together we can win*
> *With love and unity we can stand together*
> *Together we can win.*

A new sense of hope and courage filled the hearts of the people of Sanibel. They knew that together…and with God's help…they could win. They would win.

What they didn't know was that the new surge of hope that filled their hearts would be desperately needed by seven hostages who were about to begin to taste the wrath of a ruthless tormentor. With the certain impossibility of meeting the leader's demands, torture was inevitable. Three men who knew the fate of the hostages stood in the throng of cheering Sanibel citizens, hoping...praying for a miracle.

Mayor Todd whispered a prayer. "Please help us win."

A Plea to ^{CHAPTER 16} the President

As the sun made its way above the horizon, people began to stir all around Command Central. No one could be afforded the luxury of sleeping in since the fellowship hall had to be cleared of all the bedrolls and mats so that breakfast could be served.

Mary, Hazel and the breakfast crew were cooking up pancakes…hundreds of them. Partly because no new food supplies were coming on to the island and partly because the terrorists had demanded a significant quantity of supplies, food was being rationed. No one knew how long this siege might last, but they must continue to anticipate a lengthy duration.

Mayor Todd, Chief Davis and Agent Janes gathered in Central Command Headquarters (formerly Pastor Tom Johnson's office.) They knew they had to work hard and fast to make every effort to meet the demands of the Haitian commander before the hostages had suffered extreme torture.

Agent Janes began with a call to the president's office.

Using all of the influence he could as a faithful F.B.I. agent for nearly thirty years, Ron Janes pleaded with the president to expedite the return of the governor to Florida.

"Sir, seven innocent lives are on the line…and the torture will begin at sunset tonight. If the governor is not here in five days, a young internist will die."

"I'm sorry Ron. I understand your predicament. But I know you understand my dilemma as well. Iraq is complicated. The insurgents there don't think like we think. There is nothing reasonable about them."

"Sir, with all due respect, I can assure you the same is true here. These Haitian terrorists are desperate men."

"But Ron, you're talking about seven people. I'm talking about the lives of millions…about the destiny of a nation. This envoy of governors can turn the tide toward peace and stability in the entire Middle East region."

"Mr. President. I do understand. And I'm sure you understand that if we do not work with these violent captors to a place of resolution, the killing will exceed the seven hostages. While the citizens here are brave and have banded together to defend themselves, they will be no match against this ruthless adversary. It could be a bloodbath here, Sir."

"Ron, I know. I am meeting today with the Secretary of Defense. We will look at the possibility of an early departure—but don't expect the governor to come before Friday."

"Very well, sir. I do understand. May God help those hostages to endure until then."

As Agent Janes put down the phone he felt an ache in the pit of his stomach. He'd had stress in this job before, but there seemed to be more at risk in this situation.

"Friday is the best we can hope for, men. We will develop

a plan for Friday before sunset for a meeting between the governor and the Haitian Commander. Meanwhile, we'll make ready all of the other provisions."

"I have a question, Ron. You said you had an idea about the weapons. What did you have in mind?"

"Chief, I know you were involved in Desert Storm when you were a marine."

"That's right."

"You've probably fired off a few of our grenade launchers."

"Mostly in practice runs. We only got close enough to actually use them once."

"Do you remember the cotter key lock at the base of the launcher that served to prevent the mechanism from backfiring?"

"Yeah. I remember that. They warned us in training that a man could be killed if that cotter key was not secure."

Ron Janes went on. "We'll give them their twenty five launchers…and to the untrained eye, they will be in top condition. All I know is, I wouldn't want to be the man who launches that first grenade."

"Good thinking, Ron," said the mayor. "But what about the machine guns? What will you do about that?"

"We'll give them blanks, Mayor. All they'll make is noise with those things."

Chief Davis face bore heavy concern. "But what will we do when they discover they've received worthless goods?"

"We'll cross that bridge when we have to. All I know is, we simply can't put those kinds of weapons into the hands of such insanely evil men."

"Besides," the mayor broke in, "the governor will be here by the time we make any exchange and I'm hoping for some sort of break through."

Just then the phone rang. It was the Haitian Consulate.

The men were about to learn the true nature of their foes—and find a new glimmer of hope for the negotiations.

CHAPTER 17

The Haitian Connection

Agent Janes reached for the ringing phone in Pastor Tom's office. As he picked up the receiver he signaled to Chief Davis to flip the switch over to speaker phone. He sensed this would be a conversation they all would need to hear.

"Yes sir, this is Agent Janes with the F.B.I. Thank you for returning my call."

"We are glad to serve. I understand you are harboring a contingency of Haitian rebels?"

"I wouldn't put it that way."

"What do you mean, sir?"

"We are not harboring them. They have overtaken our island by force and are holding seven of our citizens as hostages. We want to know who they are and what they want."

"They are rebel scum who refused to submit to our government. They are men of deceit, thievery and murder."

Knowing something about the inner strife and governmental chaos on Haiti, it was hard for Agent Janes to discern if the men were truly rebels, or actually refugees from a hostile government. Were the men with whom they were negotiating criminals…or victims? Were they desperate for power…or desperate to escape a power that kept them in the bondage of prejudice and poverty? Even with these thoughts racing through his mind, Agent Janes knew that Haiti's civil strife was not his primary concern.

"How did these men get to our island…and why did they come?" The agent asked the consulate.

The Haitian official paused for several seconds. It was as if he were taking inventory of just how much information he should share.

"About four months ago an abandoned freighter of the French Fleet was stolen from one of our ports. The French crew had made an emergency landing here in August during the turbulence of Hurricane Ellie. Thinking the ship was no longer sea-worthy, they simply left it in our harbor giving us assurance that their government would reclaim the wreckage within the year. Since that time we have never heard anything more from their government."

"Did you try to contact the French officials?" Janes asked.

"Sir, we have a lot on our hands here. Things were difficult enough before that cursed hurricane ripped across our country. To this day we continue a recovery process. That ship was of no importance to us."

"But those rebels found it important." Agent Janes almost chided.

"Yes, they did. We estimate that approximately two hundred men boarded that ship with very few provisions, little skill and only a ghost of a chance to make it to any other tolerant port safely."

"By tolerant, you mean any port that might be sympathetic with their grievances?"

"Precisely."

"Well sir. Those men have been sailing for four months and have come ashore on the coast of Florida. They have made themselves at home on this barrier island called Sanibel. Now they have in their hands the lives of seven innocent people. What advice can you give us?"

"Do not negotiate! Attack and kill them all! They are brutal vicious men who have no sense of decency or truth. Do your best to save the hostages, but it is far better that seven should perish than hundreds die. All these men know is death and destruction...and they must be met with force."

Agent Janes listened carefully. As an investigator he had been taught to read between the lines. He knew there were multiple sides to every story. "Thank you for your help, sir. We will do the best we can."

Ron Janes slowly put down the receiver. For a few moments all three men sat in silence.

"What do you make of it, Ron? Why would a group of vicious rebels flee from a country in such haste with so little provisions?" The mayor asked.

"I don't know. From what I've read about the rebel forces in Haiti, these men don't fit the description."

"Wait a minute, men!" Interrupted Chief Davis. "These guys are violent. They have blown up our bridges, shot at the National Guard, captured a group of young girls and now are making demands for weapons and money. What do you mean they don't sound like vicious rebels?"

"You're right, Warren." The mayor agreed. "They are violent and dangerous. But I can't help but wonder if they are filled more with fear than anger. Could it be that the past four months in horrid conditions has caused these men to be desperate and confused?"

"We still don't really know who these men are. We've got to keep an open mind…and as Pastor Tom said, an open heart."

CHAPTER 18

Torture Begins

Even though there had been progress in meeting the demands of the Haitian rebels, Mayor Todd knew full well it was impossible to comply in time to spare the hostages some degree of torture. His heart was heavy as he watched the sunset. As darkness began to engulf the island, the mayor realized that a greater darkness would be flooding into the lives of seven innocent souls at the Sanibel School.

By now the Haitian commander was aware that none of his demands would be met by sunset. While he was disturbed, he was not surprised. The island leader had told him that the schedule was nearly impossible. The pleading words of the mayor rang in his ears, *please show them some mercy*. While mercy was not something the rebel leader had ever tasted, he was strangely moved to consider the mayor's plea.

The Commander barked out orders. "Bring the hostages to me!" He shouted in his native tongue of Creole. "Bring them now!"

Four men rushed to the locker room to gather the

captives to present them to their leader. Two other men swiftly made their way to a class room on the northern hall where Cindy Gray remained bound and gagged in the craft supply closet.

The seven of them were brought to the school cafeteria where they were stood in line in front of the commander.

The commander spoke with words that were firm, but somehow absent of the anger you might expect. "My friends," he said, "as of sunset tonight your people have failed to meet our demands. I made it very clear to your leader that if those stipulations were not met before the setting of the sun, your torture would begin."

At those words, young Cindy Gray gave out a whimper. Cindy had been through more than any of the other hostages. She had been held captive longer, and had spent the entire time in solitary confinement. Only twice had her abductors allowed her to drink, giving her only a few sips of water. Foolishly, both times they had removed the tape from her mouth, she had screamed, only causing the guards to quickly re-tape her.

The Commander went on; "Your leader asked for mercy. I am a fair man who has never known mercy, but I do know how to give it. If I have my men remove your gags, will you remain silent?"

They all nodded yes.

Speaking now in Creole again the leader directed his men, "Remove the tape. Get them water and food."

The guards ripped the tape from the faces of the seven prisoners. While no one spoke, each one took in several deep breaths. They welcomed the water that was brought to them, even though each was given only one small cup.

"I suggest you sip it slowly," the Commander said

with a sinister smile. "Mercy is a fleeting thing—and may not return for some time."

They sipped the water, moistening their lips, savoring every drop.

Next, the guards gave each of them a banana. While the bananas were slightly overripe, they were nutritious sustenance for the captives. Each of them was given a granola bar next, which they all recognized as coming from Hailey's store. Thinking of Hailey's Store brought some sense of normalcy—some hope for restoration.

After all seven of them had downed their granola bars, the guards were ordered to give each of them a little more water…about one third of a cup.

Slowly and with somber tone the Haitian leader spoke to his prisoners. "Tonight, you will be alone. You will be given time to think—-to reflect. You see, tomorrow when the sun is at its highest peak, if your leaders have not met my demands, mercy will run out. The torture will begin."

Once again the Commander spoke to his men. "Return the gags and take each one to a place of solitude. Strap them securely and leave them there alone in the darkness. I do not want them to have even the comfort of knowing another human is nearby."

The seven were marched out of the cafeteria in different directions. Ben was taken upstairs to the end of the north hall and tied to the sink in the janitor's closet. Cindy was returned to the school arts and crafts room. The locker room would serve as the place of confinement for Rabbi Hinman. Father Joseph and Pastor Kelso were tied in separate boys' bathrooms. Father Kline was strapped to the examination table in the nurse's office. For some odd reason, Pastor Tom Johnson was taken outside. At first he welcomed the fresh air and the night sounds, but soon the mosquitoes began to hover and strike with relentless torment. Unintentionally...perhaps...Tom's torture had begun.

The Commander had said it was to be a night for reflection. How could it be anything else? Every person knew that if no help came by mid-day tomorrow that their suffering would increase. How could anyone speculate just what a mad man might contrive as a form of torture? Would he have them beaten? Or would his attack be one against their thoughts and emotions? To some extent, they all were already in torment, yet each in his own way was reaching deep into his faith to find some comfort...some peace.

Like all of the rest, Ben thought about the possibilities that they might face. He even entertained thoughts that troops might rescue them at high noon. But he was exhausted, too tired to think anymore. Sleep. That was a solution. And so Ben Johnson allowed himself to drift off into a nightmarish sleep that brought little relief. It did, however, bring some element of escape from his horrid reality.

Ben woke up with a start. He'd heard something. It was a scraping sound at the door of the janitor's closet. He felt his heart pounding as he wondered if it were time for the torture to begin.

Slowly the closet door crept open.
"Hadid!"

CHAPTER 19

Brothers

As Ben Johnson peered into the dimly lighted hallway of the Sanibel Middle School, it was as if he were gazing upon the face of an old friend. He was so glad to see Hadid again.

Gently…quietly the young boy removed the duct tape that covered Ben's mouth.

"Thank you," Ben whispered. "It is good to see you again."

"You too, my friend." Hadid responded.

"The others? Are they okay? Have you seen any of the others?"

"Yes, they are okay. They are sleeping."

"Hadid, what do you think will happen?"

"I do not know. The Commander can be so good at times…and then almost as if possessed by some demon, he becomes cruel and violent. All I know is, your life is in danger. I want to try to help you."

"Thank you, Hadid. But I am not sure how you can help."

"I can begin with this." Hadid pulled a water bottle from a cloth bag he had strapped over his shoulder. "Drink my friend," he said, "This will bring you new strength."

"Oh, thank you, Hadid. By the way, Hadid, my name is Ben. Ben Johnson."

"Ben. That is a good name. Are you one of the Christians Elizabeth told me about back in Haiti?"

"Yes, I am Hadid. You told me that Elizabeth told you about Jesus. Are you a Christian?"

"Oh, yes. When Elizabeth told me about God's love…and how Jesus had come to earth to show us just how much God loves us, my heart was deeply touched. She showed me in the Bible about Jesus dying on the cross, being buried and three days later rising from the dead. I memorized John 3:16." The boy paused as floods of memories of special times with Elizabeth were passing though his mind. Then with tenderness Hadid recited, "For God so loved the world that He gave His only Son, that whoever believes in him should not perish, but will have everlasting life. . I knew at that very moment that Jesus was alive and that He had died on the cross for me. I surrendered my life to Him."

"That's awesome Hadid! How old were you when you began your walk with Jesus?"

"It was just last year when I was eleven."

"That's how old I was when I asked Jesus to be the lord of my life."

"We are brothers then!" Hadid said with a grin.

"Yes, we are! Brothers in Christ!"

"Ben Johnson, I want to help you escape. I am afraid there are too many guards tonight, but I will be looking for an opportunity. And Ben, I will be praying."

"Me too, my friend. You have brought me much encouragement this night. I know we will make it through this."

Hadid gave Ben a gentle hug. "I must go now. I am sorry, but I must replace the tape. I will be back when I can."

"I understand. Thank you, again, Hadid."

Hadid offered Ben one last sip of the cool water, then

he carefully secured the tape where it had been. Reluctantly the boy closed the door of Ben's prison cell and left his friend alone in the dark. Only now, the darkness was not as oppressive, for in it a ray of hope had come.

The Curse ^{CHAPTER 20}of the Island Sun

Wednesday morning came and there was still no envoy from the island leaders. The demands of the Haitian Commander were not soon to be met.

As beams of the summer sun came crashing though the windows of the middle school, the coolness of the night quickly disappeared. Each of the hostages in their solitary quarters was beginning to feel the smothering effects of the hot and humid stale air. Only Tom Johnson found the morning sun a relief, for it drove the feasting mosquitoes away from his tormented body.

Guards came to each make-shift prison cell, rushed in, released the bonds of the prisoners and gathered them together to face the commander in the cafeteria. This time, there was no sign of mercy in his expression—no hint of sympathy in his demeanor. He was hard, vicious looking, obviously enraged at the lack of response to his demands.

In his native tongue he shouted out orders to his men. The young internist was taken down the hall toward the science room. Her torment would be unique to that of the five men and young Ben Johnson. When Cindy could no longer be seen, the remaining guards stripped the six prisoners of their shirts and lined them up in front of the door that led to the play ground.

"Outside with you! Out of my sight you American scum!"

The guards guided their captives outside to the basketball court. It was a concrete slab with goals on four sides. The sun bore down relentlessly on the unshaded concrete, causing it to be burning hot to the touch.

"Lie down and burn!" The Commander pronounced from the doorway.

At that order, the guards thrust the six men with a thud to the concrete slab. They were forced to lie on the scorching stone, with their unguarded faces peering into the baking sun.

At first each of the men squirmed trying to avoid full contact with the scalding surface below them. Soon they realized, however, that the struggle was useless. After a while, they each lay quietly, helplessly receiving the searing rays on their exposed flesh.

In the beginning, sweat rolled off their bodies, providing some relief from the heat, but as dehydration invaded their bodies, the perspiration diminished and the torture became more intense. Thirst like none of them had ever known consumed their thoughts. Each breath was a laborious motion. Hearts pounded straining with the intensity of the torment.

Father Joseph, oldest of the Sanibel clergy seemed to be suffering more than the rest. His chest heaved as he wheezed in desperation. He was muttering prayers, speaking of Holy angels and the Virgin Mary. Pastor Tom knew his dear colleague and friend was in grave danger. He knew Father Joseph could not take much more of the scorching sun.

Was Ben delirious? Could he be seeing what he thought he was seeing? Out of the cafeteria door walked Hadid. As the young boy moved toward the basketball court, he removed his tattered shirt. In a gesture of compassion and solidarity with the prisoners, Hadid bravely placed himself in the scorching sun next to his new friend, Ben Johnson.

The Haitian Commander was outraged. Bursting through the door of the school cafeteria he shouted. "Stupid boy! What do you think you are doing?" With these words the leader kicked Hadid in the side. The boy did not make a sound.

With respectful defiance Hadid spoke to the ruthless Commander. "Sir. These people have done you no wrong. They are not the enemy and you know that. Why do you treat them with such cruelty?"

"You, a mere boy question my leadership? How dare you!" The commander cocked his foot in preparation to kick the boy again.

Hadid spoke quickly. "No sir. I do not question your leadership. I understand your anger. But sir, these are not the people who have wronged us!"

The Haitian leader stepped back. For a moment his eyes softened. It were as if some dark cloud had lifted. Leaving the boy lying with the rest, the Commander turned and slowly returned to the cafeteria door. Something the boy had said struck a chord. It was clear this confused and angry man found himself now deep in thought.

The sun crept slowly across the Sanibel sky sending its torturous rays relentlessly upon its victims. Father Joseph no longer muttered…his chest no longer heaved. Only a shallow, rattled breathing sound methodically made its way from the lifeless body. Was the one who began all this with an innocent prayer about to fulfill the greatest sacrifice?

It probably was a couple of hours before the suffering prisoners saw the Commander again. Hadid, like the rest, gasped for breath as the oppressive heat seemed to be suffocating them all. The boy was so thin. His physical condition was already compromised by malnutrition and the abusive hardships of the journey to America.

Why would Hadid do this? How could he endure the life-draining heat of the sun? Ben and the other men were awed by the boy's actions. They were forced to be exposed to this torture, but Hadid had laid down his life willingly. Somehow, this selfless act of Ben's new friend had softened the Commander—and ultimately would save their lives.

"Enough!" The Haitian leader appeared again in the doorway of the cafeteria. "Bring them in. Give them water."

The men were told to get up but Father Joseph didn't move. Two of the guards carried the priest into the cafeteria. Hadid struggled as well, hardly able to even hold up his head. As he entered the cafeteria, he collapsed into a heap at the feet of one of the guards. For the hostages who remained alert, the duct tape was removed and each was given sips of water.

Quietly, Tom Johnson whispered a prayer for his dear friend Joseph, then turned to the weakened Haitian boy and said, "Thank you, Hadid. Thank you."

The Real Warriors Arise

The mayor had called for another town meeting. When it was confirmed that the governor would not arrive until Friday afternoon, Mayor Todd felt the people should know the magnitude of their crisis. At 12:30 p.m. on Wednesday afternoon, the people gathered to hear the report.

"Friends," the mayor began. "Our situation is very critical. We have learned that the terrorists are Haitian rebels who left Haiti approximately four months ago on the freighter we found stranded on our shores. These men have made demands that are impossible for us to meet before Friday evening. The Haitian Commander has made it clear that if his demands are not met by sunset on Saturday, the young Cindy Gray will be killed."

At that statement, murmuring swept through the crowd. Everyone knew things were bad, but no one had any idea just how serious the situation had become.

"Furthermore," the mayor went on, "you must know

that at first the Haitian rebels wanted their demands met within thirty-six hours or they would kill the girl. We negotiated for five days to meet their request. They did say, however, that if we were unable to deliver within the thirty six hours, the hostages would be tortured."

Mary Johnson clung to her three girls at this announcement. "Girls," she said. "We've got to pray!"

"Mayor Todd." Mary Johnson spoke up from the front of the crowd. "Sir. I think we should pray."

"That's fine Mary. Perhaps later you and some others could organize a prayer meeting."

"But sir, if what you say is true, the thirty six hour time limit has expired. Our loved ones are facing torture at this very moment."

"Yes. That is true. What are you suggesting, Mary?"

"I am suggesting that everyone who feels a burden to cry out to God in behalf of the seven hostages join with me in the back parking lot under the strangler fig tree right now."

"Very well. All who feel compelled to pray, go with Mary now. I will continue my report and provide the rest of the details regarding our situation for all who remain."

A throng of praying souls made their way to the back parking lot. About half of the crowd remained to hear the mayor's report.

As soon as everyone had gathered, Mary Johnson asked the people to kneel and begin to call upon God. She encouraged them to pray specifically that God would miraculously intervene in behalf of the seven hostages.

It was 1:00 p.m. when the knees of hundreds of Sanibel citizens touched the ground, humbly calling upon a Holy, powerful God to work a miracle for their loved one.

It was precisely at 1:00 p.m., that a young Haitian boy

was strangely prompted to remove his shirt and join the ranks of the tortured at the Sanibel School.

The prayer gathering ebbed and flowed with cries for mercy, followed by words of praise. The group persevered for nearly three hours when an overwhelming peace swept over the crowd.

"Something has happened in the heavenlies!" Shouted Mary Johnson.

With tears Becky agreed. "You're right Mom. Something has changed."

A song of praise welled up from the crowd: "*All Hail the Power of Jesus' Name….*" rang through the compound. It was as if the whole Island knew that a stronghold had been broken.

But Mary knew it was not time to stop. After the hymn she addressed the praying army. "Everyone, we must continue to pray. The mayor has told us that Friday will be the crucial day of this crisis. Let's keep praying around the clock. My daughter, Kris, will draw up a sign up sheet that will cover every hour until negotiations are complete. Night and day we want to have bands of warriors praying for a true divine breakthrough.

Kris dashed to the education wing of the church building to get paper and pens. She carefully mapped out a prayer chart that would have groups of twelve praying every hour through Friday night.

Anxiously, the people lined up to get their names on the prayer chart. Like men and women signing up for military service, these prayer soldiers were ready for the battle.

Mary addressed the crowd once more. "When we know the exact time of the meeting with the Haitian rebels, we will call for a gathering here beneath the fig tree. God will go before us. Let's put our hope in Him!"

With that the throng began to sing again. This time it was "Onward Christian Soldiers." Never had such spiritual fervor moved across the island. Seeing people from all the churches, all walks of life, young and old praying in unity brought tears to Mary's eyes. While she was confident a miracle had begun at the school, she also knew that one had taken place there at Central Command.

CHAPTER 22

The Waiting Game

In a situation as intense as what the people of Sanibel faced, forty-eight hours seemed like an eternity. Magnify that reality by a thousand times, and you would have some sense of what it was like for the seven hostages.

Although the Haitian leader no longer exposed his prisoners to the torture of the sun, their blistered burned bodies created a torment that was difficult to bear. While each of them had been given small amounts of water, a veracious thirst continued to plague them. Only Cindy Gray had not been exposed to the sun. In fact, it seemed as if no new torture had been done to her.

The prisoners were no longer held in solitary confinement. All seven were secured in the school library with their duct tape removed, yet conversations forbidden.

Hadid remained with the hostages, treated as one of them by the Haitian guards.

By now, Father Joseph had shown some improvement. He was a man not only of strong character, but of physical stamina. The cool sips of water had brought new strength to the elder shepherd of Sanibel. Even though he was still in perilous condition, his warm reassuring smile brought encouragement to the rest of the captives.

Hadid, however, had not recovered from the merciless heat. Because of his weakened condition the toll of the summer sun had been more extreme on the young boy. He had become feverish, delirious and confused. It was frustrating for young Ben Johnson, who wanted to assist his friend. With hands bound, Ben, like all of the rest, was unable to provide care for the boy.

Ben did what he knew he could do. He prayed. Not only did he pray for Hadid, he prayed for the courage to do what he knew he must do. Taking a risk, he addressed the gunmen who guarded them.

"Sir, can I help him? He is dying!"

The guard looked puzzled. It was obvious he knew no English.

Cindy Gray joined the attempts to help the boy. With a fair grasp of French, another language common to Haiti, she asked, "Can the young man help the boy?"

Pleased that the young woman knew his language, the guard responded. "I will ask the Commander." At that point he left the room.

A few minutes later the Commander entered the library. "I want to know who spoke! You were forbidden to speak and you disobeyed! Whoever challenged my command—I want you to stand!"

Cindy and Ben both rose to their feet, unashamed of what they had done and unafraid of the consequences.

"Gag them!" The Commander ordered. "You will have no food—no water until I say. You must never forget. I am in charge here."

What happened next amazed them all. The Haitian

leader stepped right up into the face of Ben Johnson. "You!" He declared. "Care for the needs of the boy."

Quickly the guard untied Ben's hands. A medical kit and a pan of water were brought into the room.

"Now…help him." The commander said softly.

Ben wasn't sure what to do first, but he knew he must try to bring down the fever. He gently placed cool, damp towels on the boy's burned body. He found an ointment in the medicine kit that was specifically for burns. Lifting Hadid's head gently, Ben gave him sips of cool water to combat the dehydration.

While Ben could not speak, his eyes spoke to the eyes of Hadid. "My friend, my brother…I will help you get well."

The commander then turned to Tom Johnson and Rabbi Hinman. "You two! Come with me!"

The three men left the room. While no one knew just what might be unfolding, an atmosphere of hopefulness began to sift its way into the Sanibel School library.

The Haitian Commander took Pastor Tom and Rabbi Hinman to the principal's office. The last time Tom had found himself in the principal's office was when he was twelve—and he was in trouble then. He had slugged Billy Riley in the stomach for calling him a nerd. Because of that he had been expelled for a week. Tom hoped this visit to the principal's office would have a better outcome.

"Sit down, gentlemen. I want to talk."

Rabbi Hinman and Pastor Tom sat down in chairs in front of the principal's desk.

"I do not know what will be the conclusion of this adventure. I may have to kill you. Please understand that is not what I want to do…but we are desperate men. I have brought you here because perhaps you can help with the negotiations."

"May I speak, sir?" Tom spoke respectfully.

"Of course." The commander replied.

"How can we help?" Tom offered.

"Our people are suffering in Haiti. The government is abusive and unjust. Prejudice and corruption keep many of us in constant poverty. Daily our friends and neighbors die of disease or hunger. Unexplained kidnappings are a normal occurrence on the streets of Port au Prince. We have petitioned our leaders for justice—for help, but they have branded us as rebels and traitors."

The Rabbi spoke next. "We know that Haiti has suffered much and has been in great turmoil. Much of our help from the United States has been met with resistance."

"Then you do understand." The Commander went on. "We learned from one of your missionaries of the wealth of America. She spoke of caring people who would help us. Hoping to find some assistance, we stole an old freighter and made our way to your country."

"The ship on the beach?"

"Yes. We nearly all died. Conditions were horrible. We had so little food. Only a handful of us knew anything about sailing a freighter ship. Some did die. One morning I found a man who had gone mad devouring the flesh of one of the other men. I too was affected by the ravaging heat and the persistent, tumbling waves. By the time we landed on your shore we were prepared to take whatever measures it required to get help for our people."

"Sir, perhaps it is not too late to try peaceful means. We can help you." Pastor Tom suggested.

"Perhaps." The Commander pondered. But before he could speak another word a sound arose in the distance.

"*Honk! Honk!….Honk! Honk!*"

A large white van and a mid-sized truck were positioned at the negotiation point. Inside the van were Mayor Todd, Agent Janes, Chief Davis and the governor. Hidden in the back seat of the van were two F.B.I. marksmen with M-16's prepared to take out the Haitian leader with a single shot if negotiations failed.

CHAPTER 23
Breakthrough

The governor had arrived sooner than expected. Talks in Iraq had been productive, and with relations strengthening, several members of the U.S. delegation had been able to come home early.

Knowing the urgency of the situation, the governor had flown directly to Fort Myers. A small boat hailing a white flag had brought the governor to the Sanibel shore. What the Haitian gunmen guarding the shore did not detect were the two F.B.I. sharpshooters, one captaining the boat, the other appearing to be the governor's secretary.

Attribute it to good fortune, or simply to the diligent effort of government officials, but Mary Johnson and her army of prayer warriors were giving God the credit for the positive turn of events. Negotiations were going to take place on Thursday, not Friday. It was 2:00 p.m. when the governor, along with the mayor, police chief and Agent Janes made their way to the Sanibel School.

As the van departed Command Central, Mary rallied the people to pray. Gathering again under the huge strangler fig in the rear parking lot of Community Church, several hundred Sanibel citizens knelt to pray.

"Pray for a peaceful end to this crisis." Mary encouraged.

A man spoke up from the middle of the crowd. "Pray for wisdom for the governor and our mayor."

"Pray for the hostages to be set free unharmed." A woman spoke up from the rear of the throng.

Passionate prayers ascended to the throne of God.

While the people prayed, the governor laid out a plan to the riders in the van.

"Only the mayor and I will meet with the Haitian leader."

A voice from the back seat asked, "Do you both have on your bullet proof vests?"

"Yes." The governor replied. He continued. "The weapons they have requested, as well as the funds are secure in the truck behind us. Before any of those items are transferred to the Haitians, I plan to negotiate for a surrender. Let's hope this thing comes to an end today."

As Agent Janes drove the van up to the negotiation point, he honked the horn. That was the mutually agreed upon signal the negotiations would be resumed.

From the front doors of Sanibel Middle School emerged the Commander, surrounded by about a dozen armed men. Much to Mayor Todd's surprise, the Haitian leader was also accompanied by Pastor Tom Johnson and Rabbi Hinman.

The mayor quickly noticed the sun-burned blistered skin of his two friends. He was pleased, however, to observe no other obvious harm that the two had suffered.

The Haitian commander was the first to speak. "Governor, my name is Jean Bardeaux. I am the leader of this company of brave Haitian men."

"Mr. Bardeaux. What do you want from us?"

"I want to help my people back in Haiti. I want fifty million dollars and transportation to take me and my men safely back to Haiti. Furthermore, I want your assurance that there will be no actions taken against us. We must return as free men in good standing with your government and ours."

"Sir, I do not have the authority to grant you full amnesty. That would require an act of the president."

At that remark, the commander became sullen, yet he did not seem angry.

"Mr. Governor. I understand powers and authorities. I know there are certain limitations to what you can do."

At that moment Tom Johnson spoke. "Mr. Bardeaux, may I share a word with the governor?"

"Very well. Speak."

"Sir, thank you for your commitment to resolving this incident with peaceful negotiations. I assure you that is the desire of Mr. Bardeaux." Pastor Tom made a rather bold statement, because he wasn't really sure the Haitian Commander was as committed to a peaceful process.

"What are you suggesting, pastor? The governor asked.

"Rabbi Hinman and I have been listening to the serious grievances of Commander Bardeux and his men. I am convinced and would be willing to testify, that he and his men have a justifiable case that should come before a United Nations Human Rights Committee."

The Rabbi nodded in agreement. "While these men have demonstrated some violent behaviors at the onset of this encounter, deep down I do not believe them to be men of criminal character. They have treated us acceptably, and I too would be willing to testify in their behalf."

It was as if both men had forgotten the hours in the scorching sun on the concrete slab…or the days with little food or water. Were they somehow confused because of the torture—or were they compassionate because they genuinely sensed that this horror story could have a happy ending?

"Mr. Bardeaux." The governor spoke deliberately. "Here is what I can promise you: If your men will surrender and turn in all of their weapons, I will guarantee that you have your day in court. Not only will these good pastors testify in your behalf, but I personally will join them."

The mayor broke in. "If it will help, I will testify also."

Even Chief Davis who had regarded the Haitians as brutal rebels was willing to help.

"Sir," the governor went on, "Puerto Rico is a neutral territory for such cases. We will see that you and your men are well cared for, transported safely and held under only minimum security until this issue is resolved."

"What about the fifty million dollars?" The Commander said firmly. "Can you promise we will get the help we need for our people?"

The governor paused, selecting his words carefully. "I can only promise you that I will do everything I can within my power to get your people all the assistance I can. I personally will oversee the distribution of any assistance so that it does not pass through the hands of corrupt government officials."

Almost as if he were relieved as all of the rest, the Haitian leader gave out a long sigh. "Very well. We will surrender. I will send word to our men along the shorelines to retreat. We will lay down our weapons."

"I will make calls immediately to assure your safe transport to Puerto Rico as well as arrange professional medical care for you and all of your men." The governor spoke with calm assurance to the Haitian Commander. Without compromise, he had been able to steer the negotiations to a conclusion that would be a good solution for all.

Pastor Tom stepped forward and extended his hand to

the governor. "Thank you sir. We are forever indebted to you for your commitment to justice." The pastor then pivoted and reached out to offer that same firm handshake to Commander Bardeaux. "Thank you, sir, for your willingness to allow the justice system to have due process."

It was at that point that the pastor's eyes welled up with tears. "Now sir, I beg you. Please release my son and the others and let us go free."

A tear streamed down the cheek of the Commander. "You are free. Go quickly to your friends."

Tom Johnson rushed to the Sanibel School library to tell the others the good news. They were free. The crisis was over. For a long moment Pastor Tom clung to his son.

"Ben, thank God you're alright."

Cindy Gray just sat in one of the wooden library chairs and sobbed.

Rabbi Hinman, Father Kline and Pastor Kelso gathered around their friend, Father Joseph, preparing to carry him to the waiting van. The old priest was doing much better, but he was still too weak to walk.

"Dad!" Ben exclaimed. "What about Hadid? He is very sick. I've tried to bring the fever down, but he's still burning up."

"We'll get him help, son."

By now Hadid was unconscious. His breathing was labored—the relentless fever ravaged his body. The boy must have help—and it must come very soon.

What About Hadid?

CHAPTER 24

As the white van pulled into Command Central that afternoon, the crowd of citizens swarmed around it, anxious for a report. As soon as they saw that the van was crowded now with seven new passengers, a shout went up from the people.

"I see them!" Someone shouted. "They're all there. All seven of them!"

Mary began to sob. Becky, Kris and Marty stood close by their mother, tears streaming as they watched Tom and Ben emerge from the van. Then they ran...as fast as they could run, breaking their way thoughtlessly through the mob...toward their men.

"Let 'em through!" A voice yelled.

The crowd parted reminiscent of the Red Sea allowing the mother and three daughters to make their way to their loved ones.

With their sunburned bodies, Tom and Ben both remembered them as the most painful, wonderful hugs they had ever had. They were free and back with their family. At that moment, that's all that really mattered.

The mayor made his way to the top of the van and from there he addressed the happy crowd. "Citizens of Sanibel. Our siege is over!"

Cheers rose up in thunderous response to the mayor's words. For several minutes the air was filled with shouts and applause.

"Please listen everyone." The mayor pleaded, trying to quiet the crowd. "I want to tell you how this all came to an end. Our good governor came as quickly as possible and negotiated a peaceful settlement with our intruders."

Again the crowd celebrated, expressing appreciation to the governor for the work he had done. The governor waved and nodded his head acknowledging his gratitude for their applause.

The mayor went on with his remarks. "We thought we had been overcome by violent rebels who were out to plunder our island. It seems that what we have actually faced is a band of desperate refugees from Haiti, seeking to find relief for their people."

The crowd grew quiet. Many felt a sense of shame for the hatred they had allowed to rise up within them without really knowing the whole story.

"Please understand," the mayor spoke with assurance. "These men will face a United Nations hearing to determine retribution for their crimes against Sanibel. With that hearing, however, their own grievances will be heard regarding the abusive oppression in their homeland."

Everyone was pleased that the men would receive due legal process and that justice would be served.

A tragedy had been averted. In fact, there seemed to be a redemptive thread woven throughout the entire crisis.

Sanibel would be even stronger—more united. The pastors and churches would find a new spirit of cooperation. Neighbors had become friends. A new and deeper faith in God had spread throughout the island. And hopefully, a band of brave Haitians would find hope for their people.

"But what about Hadid?" Ben interrupted the mayor.

"Do you mean the young Haitian boy?"

"Yes, that is Hadid. He saved our lives."

Agent Janes quickly climbed to the top of the van. "The young boy has been life-flighted to Southwest Regional Hospital. He is in critical condition. Ben, he is asking for you. We want to get you to him immediately!"

The agent jumped from the van and made his way to Ben Johnson. "Ben, come with me…now!"

At that moment the sound of an approaching chopper filled the air. Young Ben Johnson would experience his first helicopter ride with the hope of saving the life of one who had saved him.

The National Guard Special Unit helicopter landed gently on the pad at Southwest Regional Hospital. Even before the prop had fully stopped, Ben was escorted to the emergency room. There he found his friend surrounded by care-givers, hooked to what seemed like a dozen machines sustaining his life.

"Are you Ben?" A doctor asked.

"Yes, how did you know my name?"

"That is the only word he has spoken. Ben, let him know you are here. Take his hand and tell him he is going to be alright."

"Hadid. My friend…my brother. It's Ben. Hadid, you are going to be alright."

The boy gave a slight squeeze to Ben's hand and managed a smile through all of the tubes and wires hooked to his frail body. While Hadid could not speak, it was clear the presence of his friend brought encouragement.

"God, please don't let him die." Ben whispered, as he made his way out the large intensive care unit doors.

It was only a few moments later when Tom, Mary, Becky, Kris and Marty came into the small hospital waiting room.

"Son," Mary spoke with assurance. We have called upon the whole Island to pray. We've told people to send out e-mails—call their families and friends. We've rallied a prayer support for your friend that is spreading around the world."

Ben found great comfort in his mother's words… and in her faith.

Tom Johnson put his arm around Ben's shoulders. "Son, let's pray now."

The family knelt together in the waiting room, transforming it into a prayer chapel. Pastor Tom prayed, "Father, you are the God who gives and takes away. You are holy, just and merciful. Blessed be your name. We cry out to you for our young friend. Please help him. Please heal him. Just as your son lay down his life for us, Hadid lay down his life to save us. Thank you for such great love. We put him in your merciful hands, O God—and we entrust him to your care. In Jesus Name. Amen."

"Amen." Ben said quietly. "I'm going back in with him. I want to stay as long as they will let me stay."

Quietly, Ben made his way back to the bedside of young Hadid. As he took the boy's hand, he noticed it was no longer as hot as it had been.

Ben spoke with assurance. "Hadid. Hadid. You're going to be alright. Thousands are praying for you. God is with you."

Hadid opened his eyes. They were eyes that sparkled

with renewed hope. A large grin covered the boy's face. This time Hadid squeezed Ben's hand firmly as if to say, "You're right."

And Ben was right. Miraculous would be the only way to describe the young boy's recovery.

Ten days later, Hadid emerged from Southwest Regional. Bathed in prayer, with replenished fluids, nutritious meals and strong antibiotics to drive away the infection from his ravaged body, Hadid had regained his strength.

What Hadid did not know was that while doctors were working with him, the Johnsons were working with the Haitian government. Hadid was no longer an orphan.

The two boys embraced, declaring a truth that actually began in the dark hallway of the Sanibel School. "Brother!" they shouted together with joy.

QUESTIONS FOR REFLECTION

1. What made the people of Sanibel Island so fearful of their invaders?
2. Why do you think the pastors were willing to make the exchange?
3. Were the invaders evil?
4. How was Hadid different from all of the other invaders?
5. What are some things Ben did wrong? What are some things Ben did right?
6. What could the invaders have done differently to achieve their goals?
7. What do you think really made the difference in how the story ended?

WHAT MADE HADID DIFFERENT?

Question number four asked, "How was Hadid different from all of the other invaders?" It is clear that a personal relationship with Jesus Christ was the difference in his life. While others were without hope, Hadid was optimistic. When the commander and his men sought vengeance, Hadid was pursuing friendships. With others defending their lives...or seeking to destroy the lives of others, Hadid was willing to lay down his life for his friends. Jesus Christ is the One who empowered Hadid to live that way.

Do you have a life-changing relationship with Jesus Christ? He made it simple for us to get to know Him...to experience abundant life now...and eternal life to come.

It is as simple as ABC.

A=Acknowledge that you need Him and want Him in your life.

B=Believe that Jesus died on the cross and rose again for your salvation.

C=Commit your life to Him. Confess Him as Lord, and submit to His leadership.

Simply tell God you are sorry for your sins, and thank

Him for sending His Son to die in your place. Repent, or turn from any sin that you know of in your life that is not pleasing to God. Put your trust (believe) in what Jesus has done for you on the cross. Invite Him to come into your life and change your life, as Lord of your life.

And now, tell someone that Jesus is now Lord of your life. Find a good church that loves Jesus and honors His Word, the Bible. Grow in Christ, and you will grow in joy, peace and purposeful living!